LUKE PEARSON

HILDA
AND
THE STONE FOREST

FLYING EYE BOOKS
LONDON | NEW YORK

THIS BOOK BELONGS TO

FOR PHILIPPA

SPECIAL THANKS TO PHILIPPA RICE, EVERYONE AT NOBROW AND FLYING EYE, EM PARTRIDGE, JON MCNAUGHT, BJORN RUNE LIE, HANNA K, KURT MUELLER AND ALL MY FAMILY AND FRIENDS.

THIS PAPERBACK EDITION PUBLISHED IN 2018. FIRST PUBLISHED IN 2016 BY FLYING EYE BOOKS, AN IMPRINT OF NOBROW LTD. 27 WESTGATE STREET, LONDON E8 3RL.

2 4 6 8 10 9 7 5 3 1

PUBLISHED IN THE US BY NOBROW (US) INC.

PRINTED IN POLAND ON FSC® CERTIFIED PAPER.

ISBN: 978-1-911171-71-3

MIX
Paper from responsible sources
FSC www.fsc.org FSC® C001693

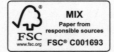

ORDER FROM WWW.FLYINGEYEBOOKS.COM

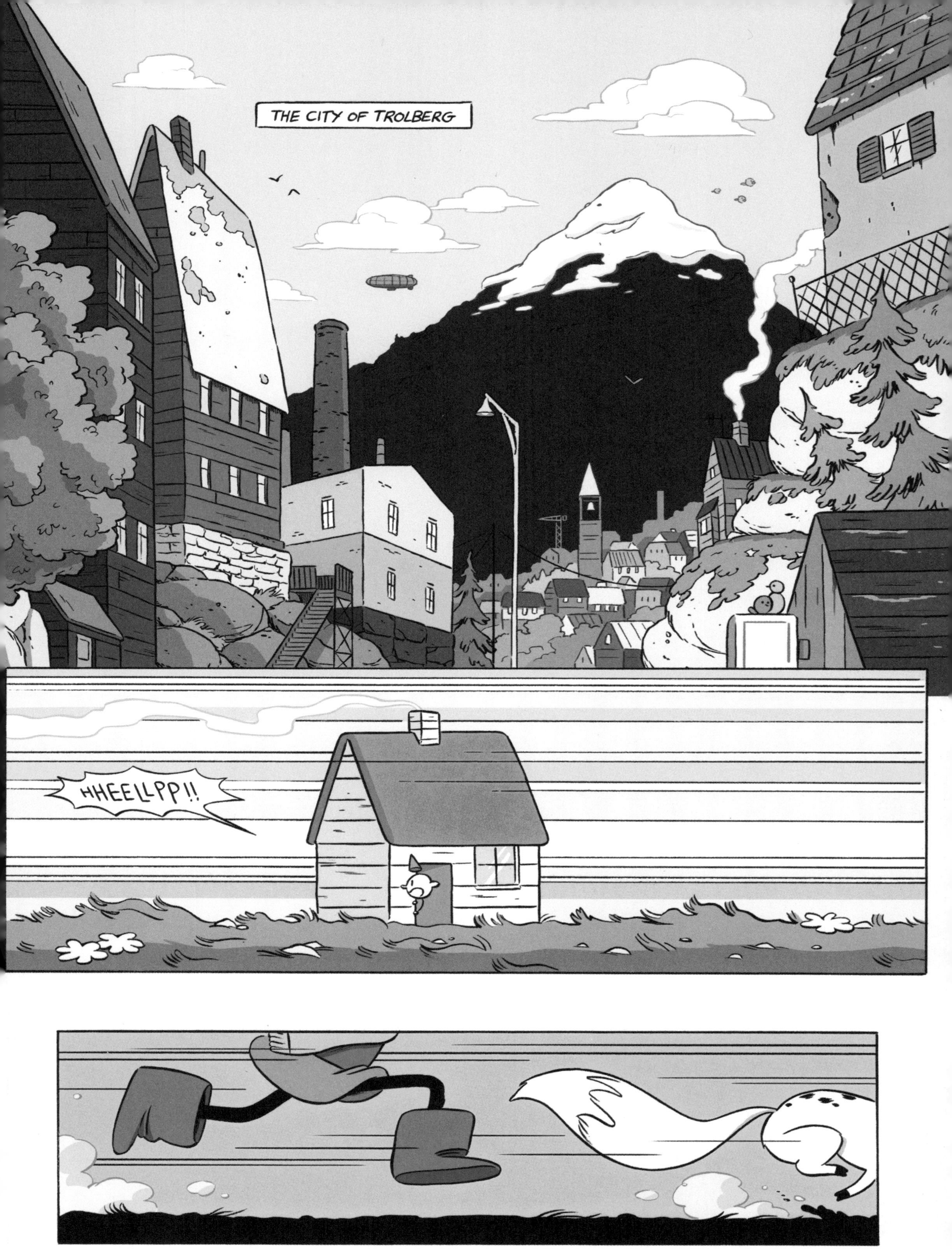
THE CITY OF TROLBERG
HHEELLPP!!

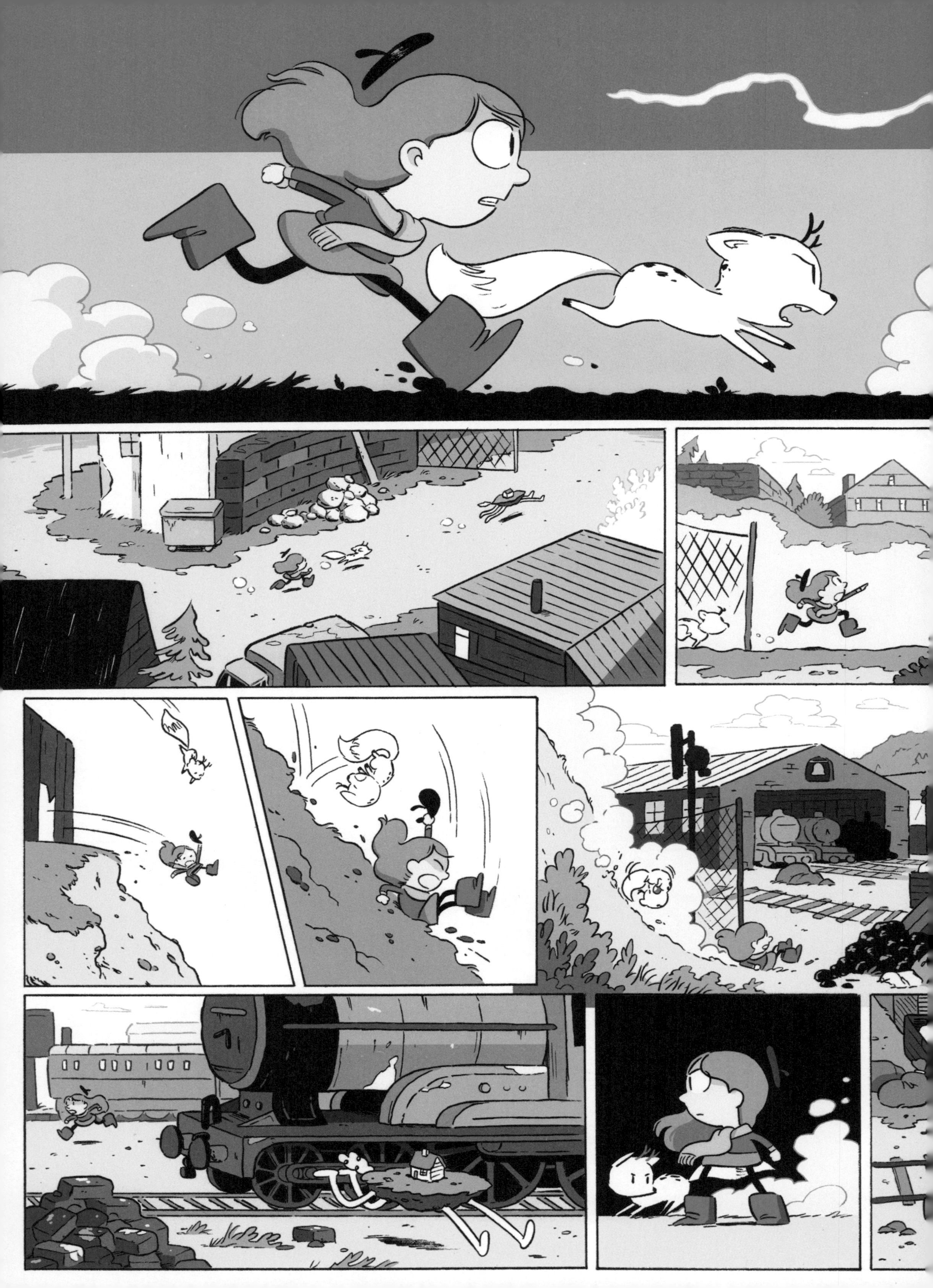

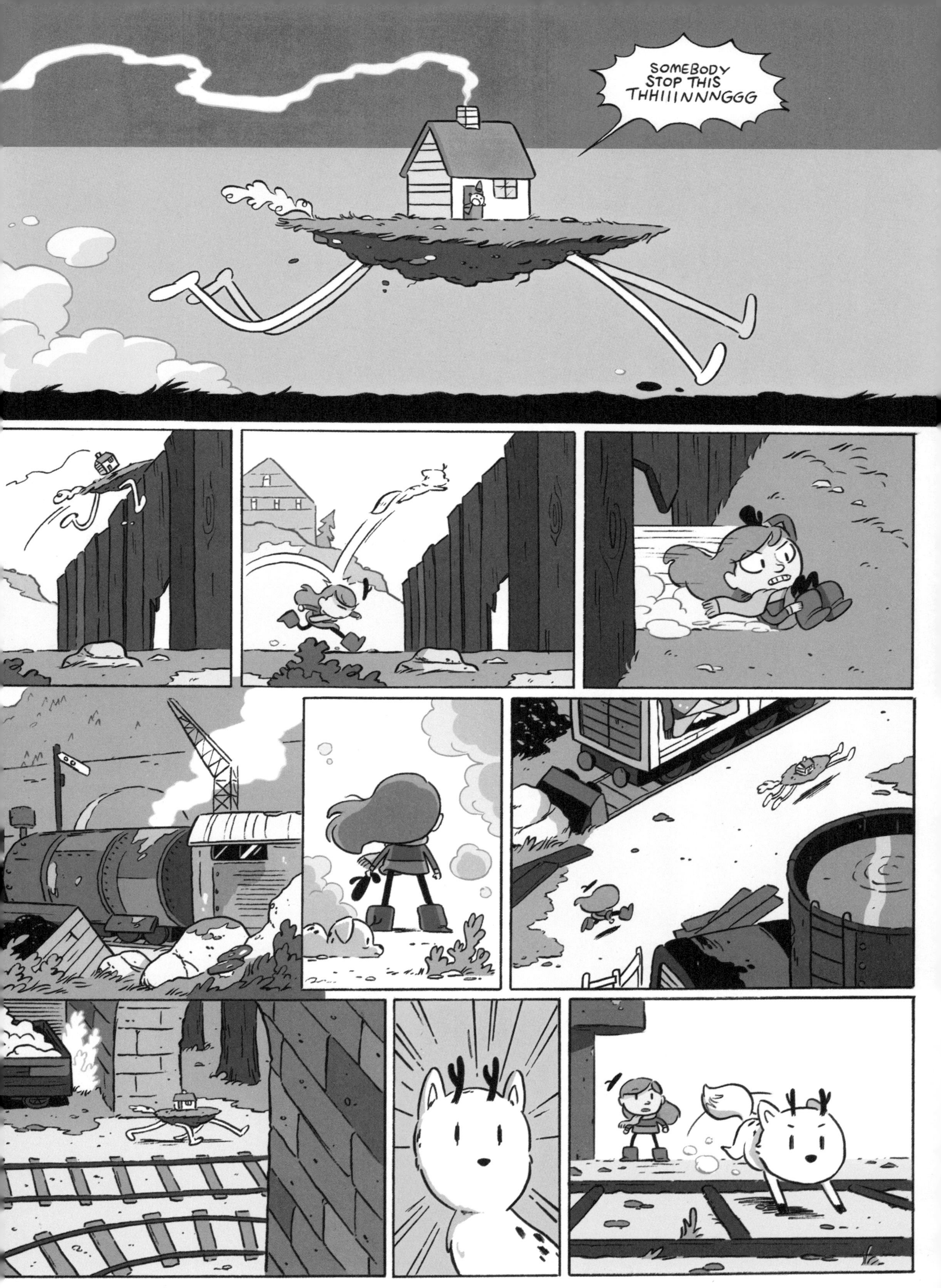
SOMEBODY STOP THIS THHIIINNNGGG

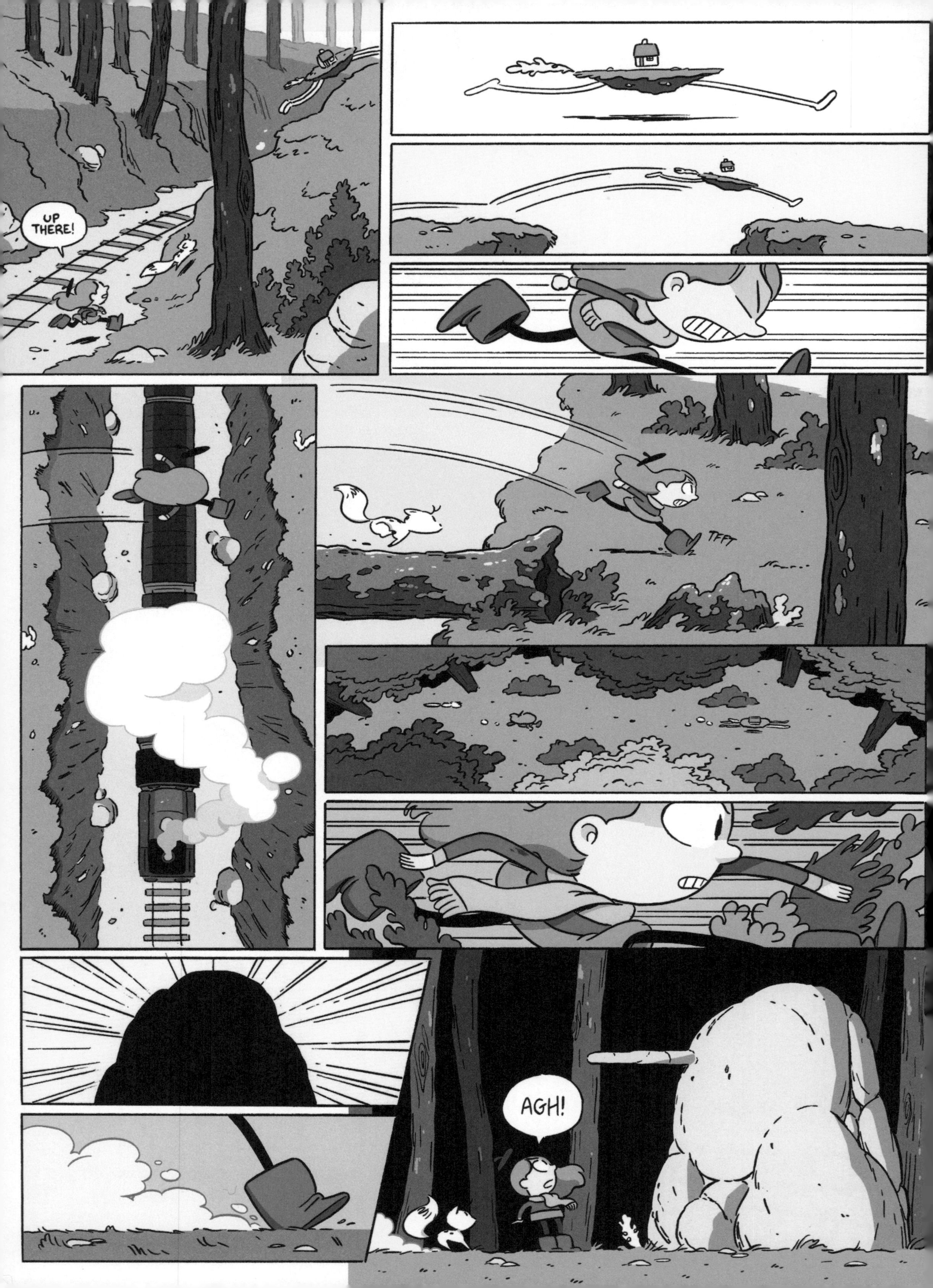
UP THERE!
TFFT
AGH!

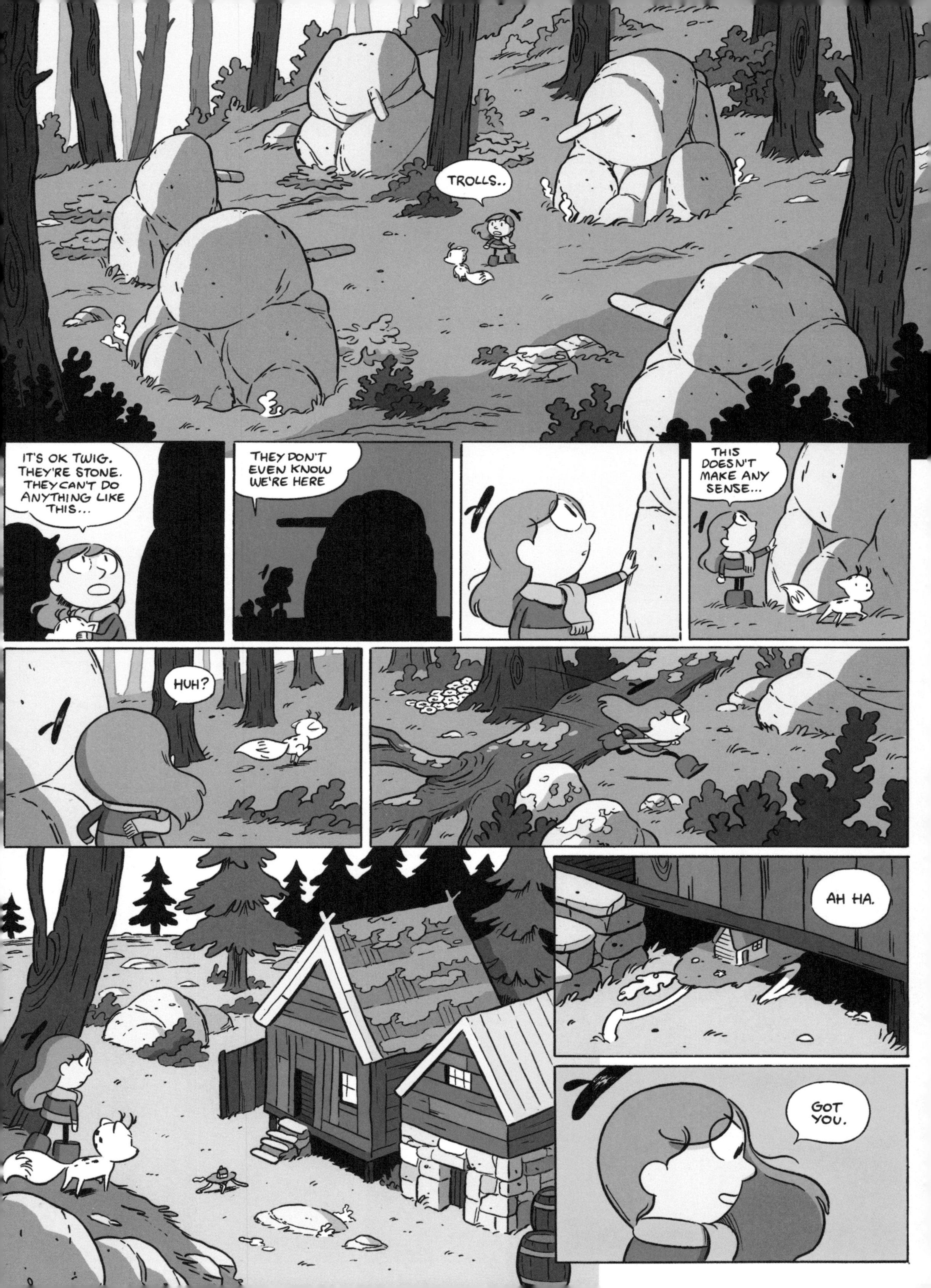

TROLLS..
IT'S OK TWIG. THEY'RE STONE. THEY CAN'T DO ANYTHING LIKE THIS...
THEY DON'T EVEN KNOW WE'RE HERE
THIS DOESN'T MAKE ANY SENSE...
HUH?
AH HA.
GOT YOU.

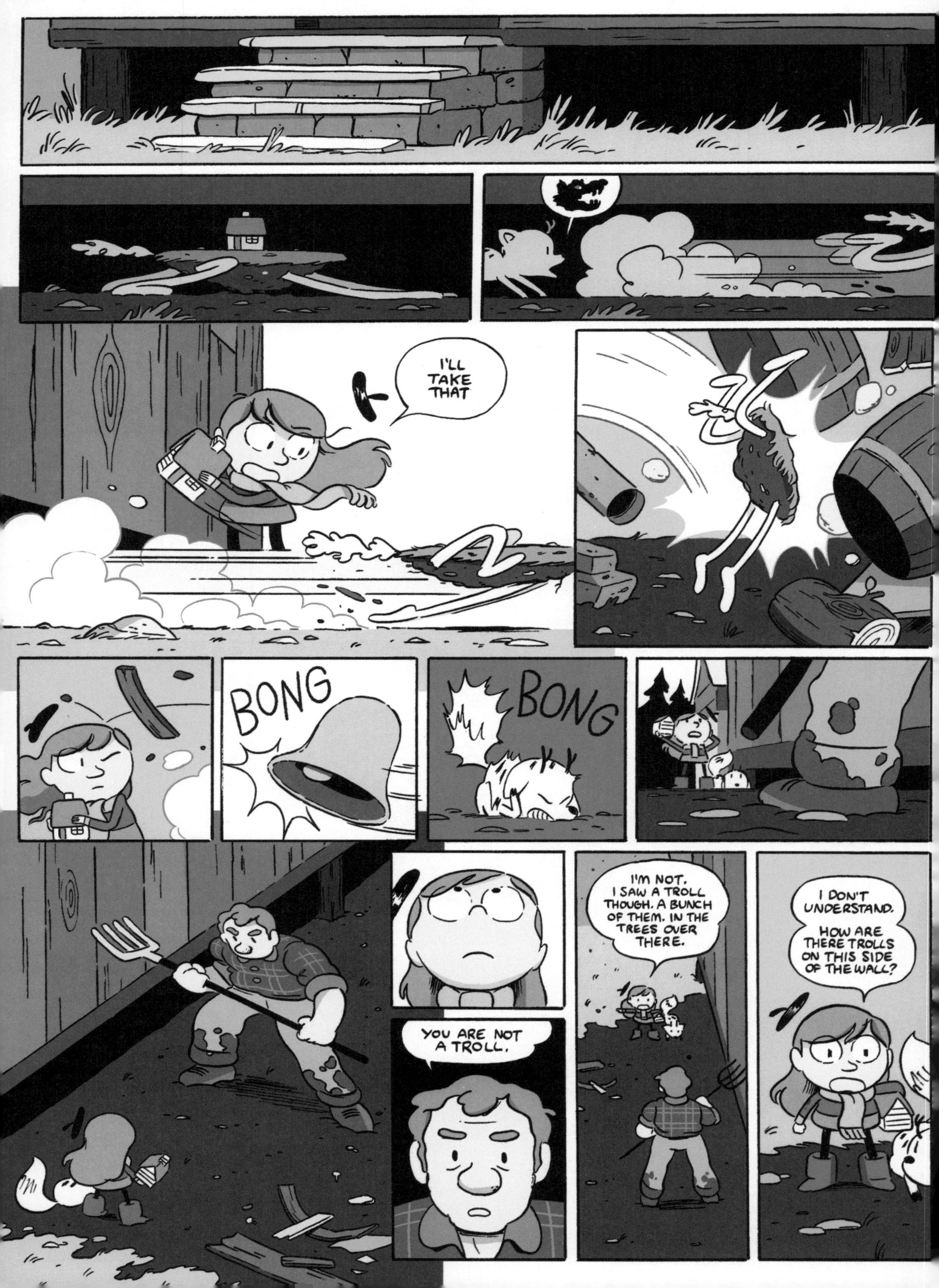
I'LL TAKE THAT
BONG
BONG
I'M NOT. I SAW A TROLL THOUGH. A BUNCH OF THEM. IN THE TREES OVER THERE.
YOU ARE NOT A TROLL.
I DON'T UNDERSTAND.
HOW ARE THERE TROLLS ON THIS SIDE OF THE WALL?

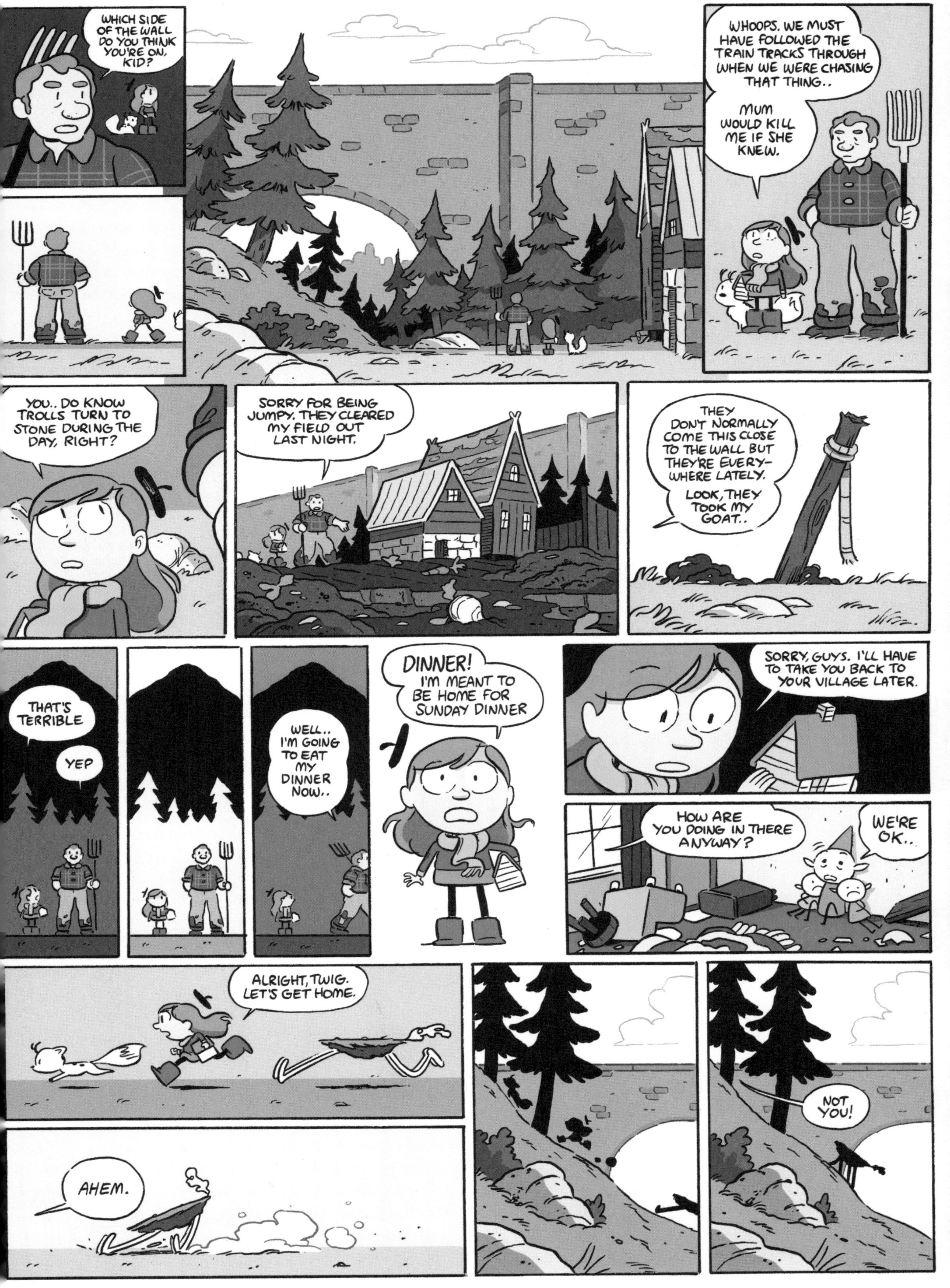
WHICH SIDE OF THE WALL DO YOU THINK YOU'RE ON, KID?
WHOOPS. WE MUST HAVE FOLLOWED THE TRAIN TRACKS THROUGH WHEN WE WERE CHASING THAT THING..
MUM WOULD KILL ME IF SHE KNEW.
YOU.. DO KNOW TROLLS TURN TO STONE DURING THE DAY, RIGHT?
SORRY FOR BEING JUMPY. THEY CLEARED MY FIELD OUT LAST NIGHT.
THEY DON'T NORMALLY COME THIS CLOSE TO THE WALL BUT THEY'RE EVERY-WHERE LATELY.
LOOK, THEY TOOK MY GOAT..
THAT'S TERRIBLE
YEP
WELL.. I'M GOING TO EAT MY DINNER NOW..
DINNER! I'M MEANT TO BE HOME FOR SUNDAY DINNER
SORRY, GUYS. I'LL HAVE TO TAKE YOU BACK TO YOUR VILLAGE LATER.
HOW ARE YOU DOING IN THERE ANYWAY?
WE'RE OK..
ALRIGHT, TWIG. LET'S GET HOME.
AHEM.
NOT YOU!

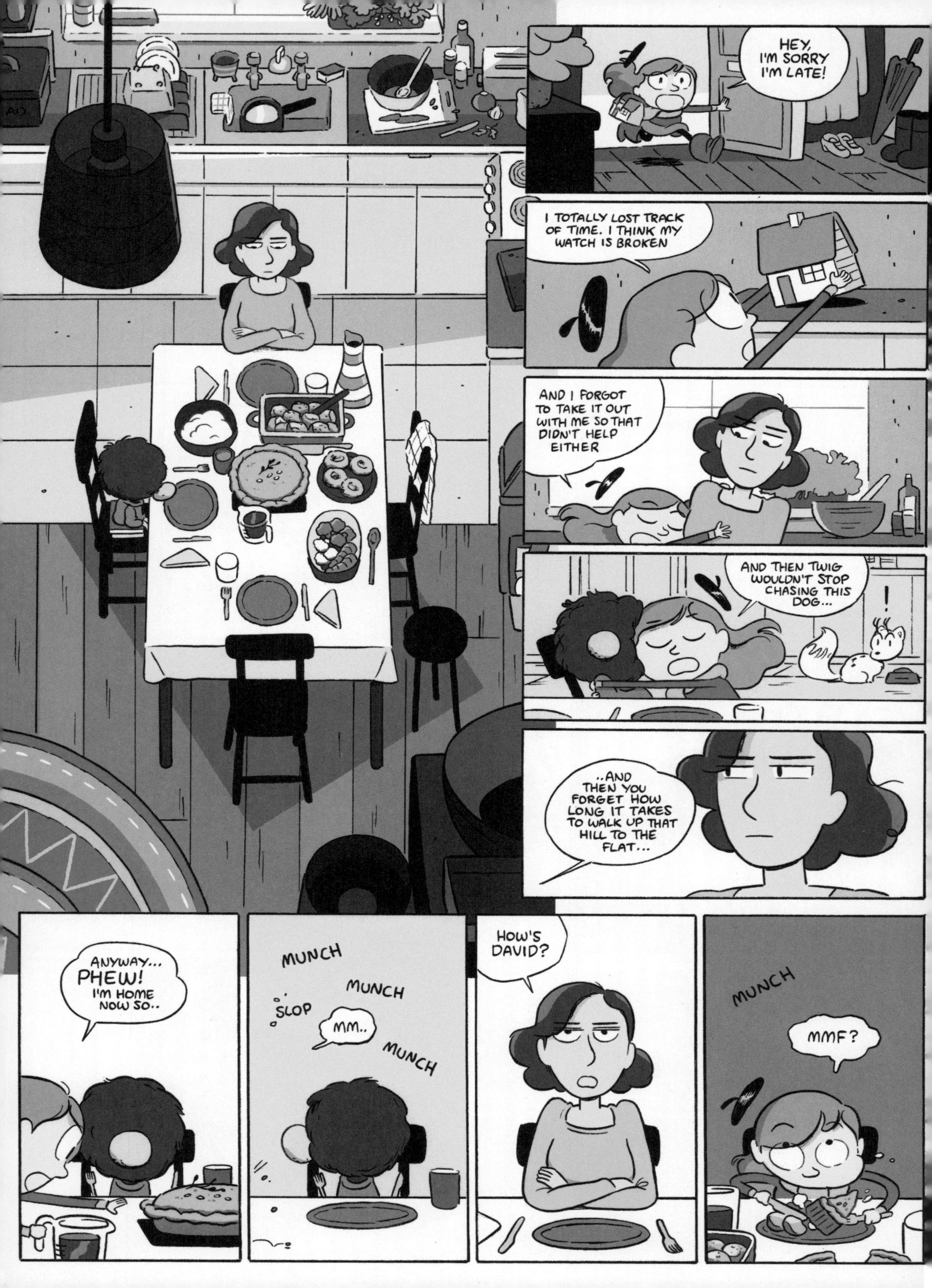
HEY, I'M SORRY I'M LATE!
I TOTALLY LOST TRACK OF TIME. I THINK MY WATCH IS BROKEN
AND I FORGOT TO TAKE IT OUT WITH ME SO THAT DIDN'T HELP EITHER
AND THEN TWIG WOULDN'T STOP CHASING THIS DOG...
!
..AND THEN YOU FORGET HOW LONG IT TAKES TO WALK UP THAT HILL TO THE FLAT...
ANYWAY... PHEW! I'M HOME NOW SO..
MUNCH
MUNCH
SLOP
MM..
MUNCH
HOW'S DAVID?
MUNCH
MMF?

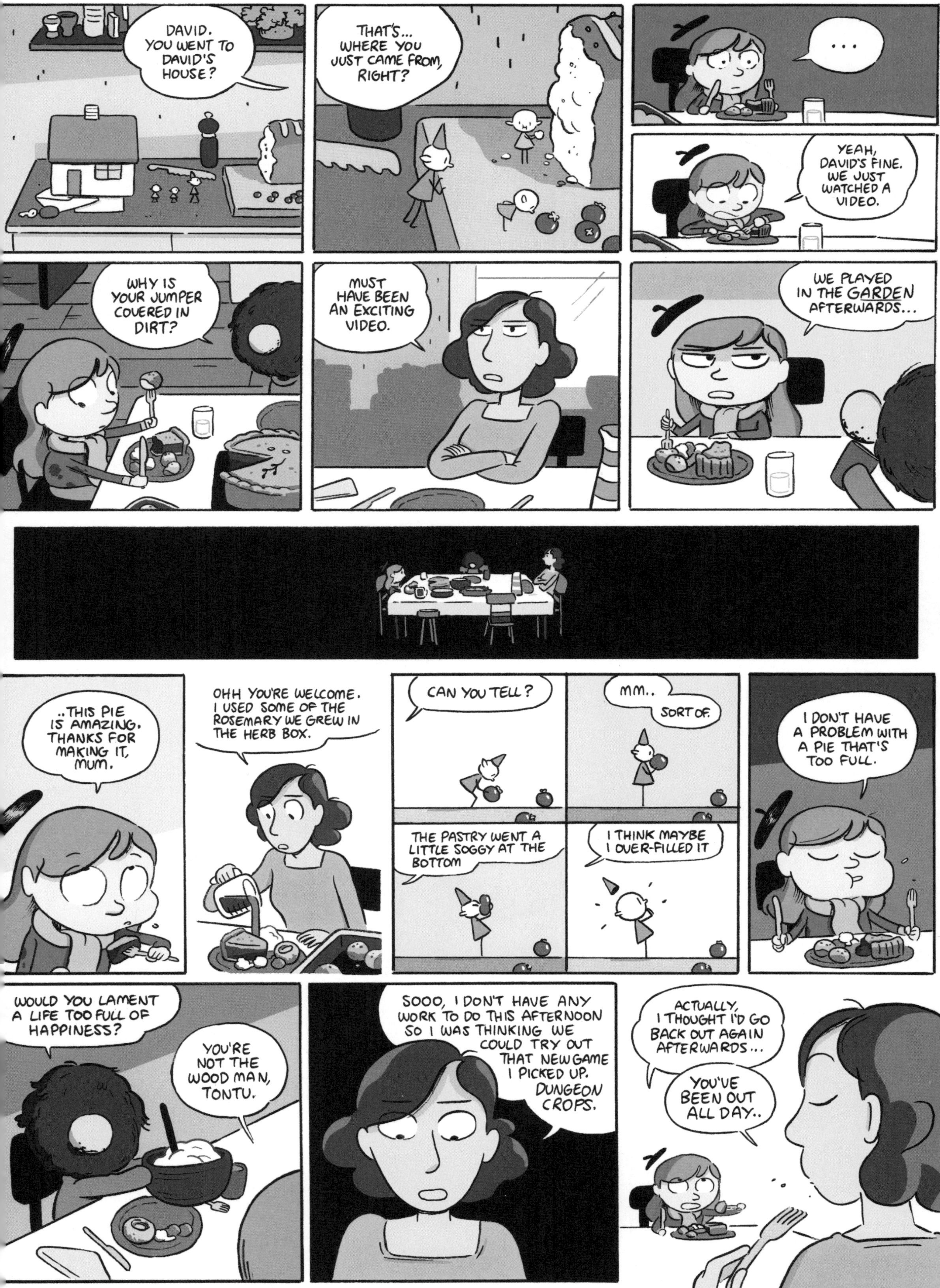
DAVID. YOU WENT TO DAVID'S HOUSE?
THAT'S... WHERE YOU JUST CAME FROM, RIGHT?
...
YEAH, DAVID'S FINE. WE JUST WATCHED A VIDEO.
WHY IS YOUR JUMPER COVERED IN DIRT?
MUST HAVE BEEN AN EXCITING VIDEO.
WE PLAYED IN THE GARDEN AFTERWARDS...
..THIS PIE IS AMAZING. THANKS FOR MAKING IT, MUM.
OHH YOU'RE WELCOME. I USED SOME OF THE ROSEMARY WE GREW IN THE HERB BOX.
CAN YOU TELL?
MM..
SORT OF.
THE PASTRY WENT A LITTLE SOGGY AT THE BOTTOM
I THINK MAYBE I OVER-FILLED IT
I DON'T HAVE A PROBLEM WITH A PIE THAT'S TOO FULL.
WOULD YOU LAMENT A LIFE TOO FULL OF HAPPINESS?
YOU'RE NOT THE WOOD MAN, TONTU.
SOOO, I DON'T HAVE ANY WORK TO DO THIS AFTERNOON SO I WAS THINKING WE COULD TRY OUT THAT NEW GAME I PICKED UP. DUNGEON CROPS.
ACTUALLY, I THOUGHT I'D GO BACK OUT AGAIN AFTERWARDS...
YOU'VE BEEN OUT ALL DAY..

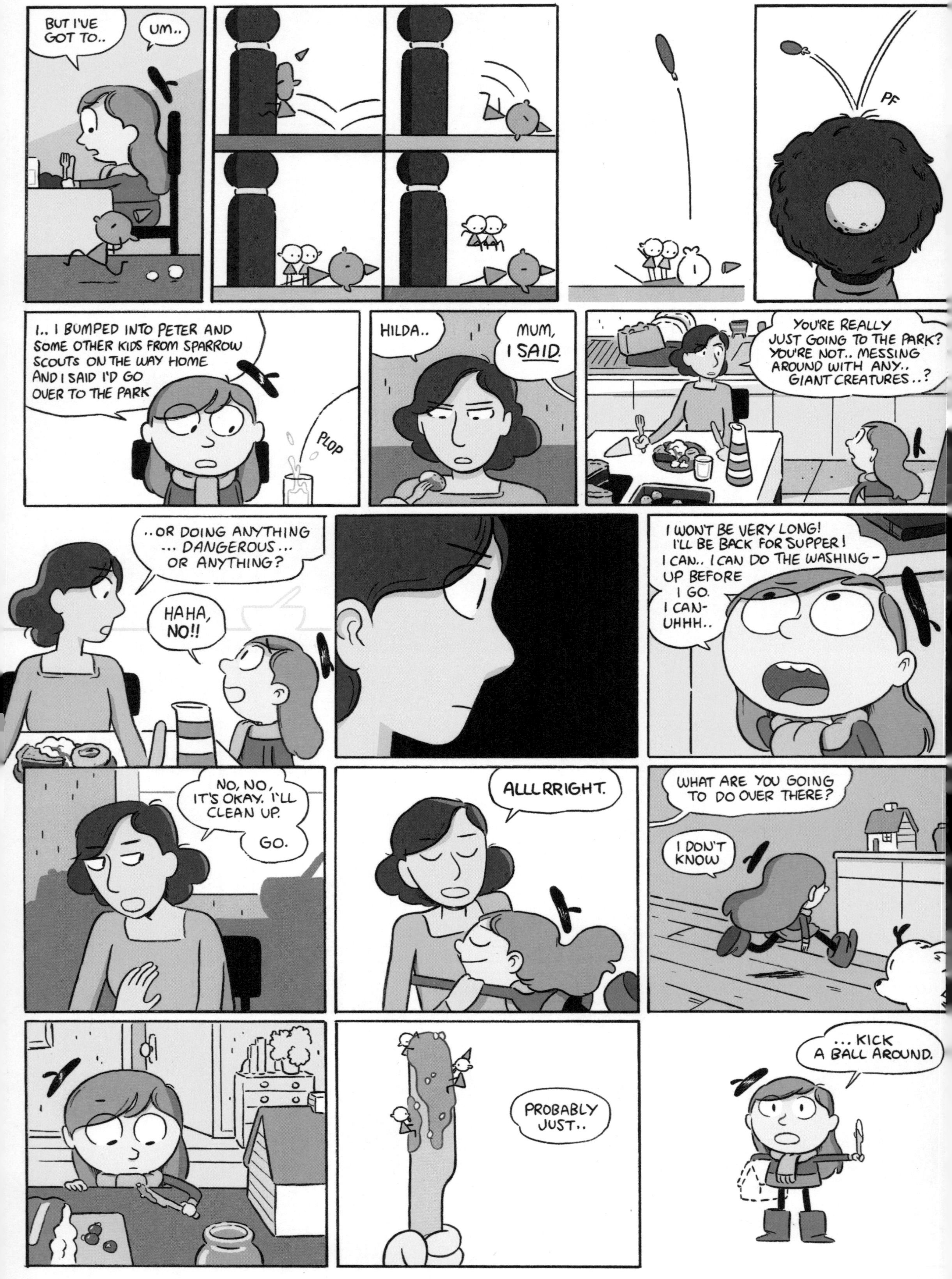
BUT I'VE GOT TO..
UM..
PF
I.. I BUMPED INTO PETER AND SOME OTHER KIDS FROM SPARROW SCOUTS ON THE WAY HOME AND I SAID I'D GO OVER TO THE PARK
PLOP
HILDA..
MUM, I SAID.
YOU'RE REALLY JUST GOING TO THE PARK? YOU'RE NOT.. MESSING AROUND WITH ANY.. GIANT CREATURES..?
..OR DOING ANYTHING ... DANGEROUS... OR ANYTHING?
HAHA, NO!!
I WON'T BE VERY LONG! I'LL BE BACK FOR SUPPER! I CAN.. I CAN DO THE WASHING-UP BEFORE I GO. I CAN- UHHH..
NO, NO, IT'S OKAY. I'LL CLEAN UP.
GO.
ALLLRRIGHT.
WHAT ARE YOU GOING TO DO OVER THERE?
I DON'T KNOW
PROBABLY JUST..
... KICK A BALL AROUND.

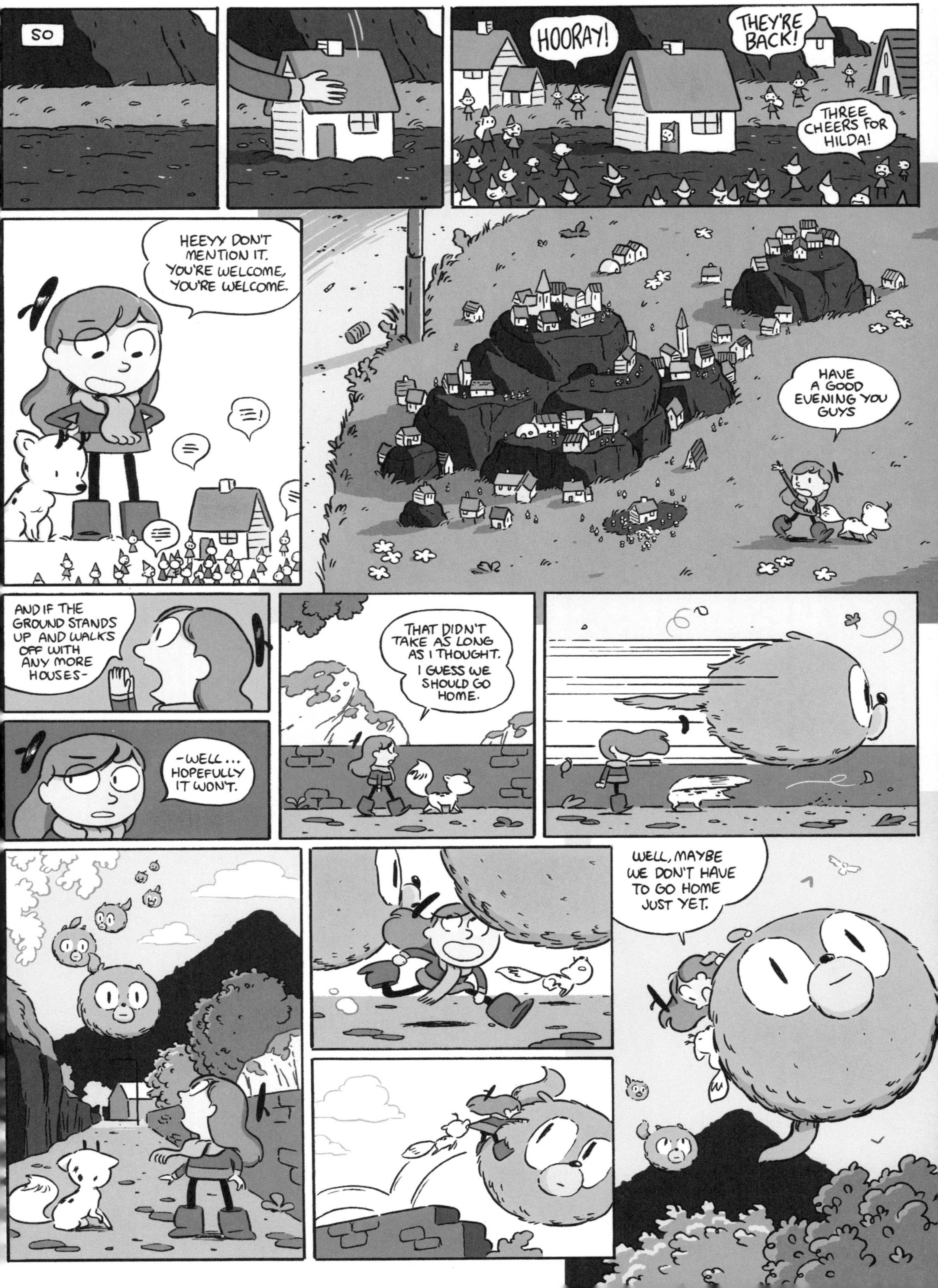
SO
HOORAY!
THEY'RE BACK!
THREE CHEERS FOR HILDA!
HEEYY DON'T MENTION IT. YOU'RE WELCOME, YOU'RE WELCOME.
HAVE A GOOD EVENING YOU GUYS
AND IF THE GROUND STANDS UP AND WALKS OFF WITH ANY MORE HOUSES-
-WELL... HOPEFULLY IT WON'T.
THAT DIDN'T TAKE AS LONG AS I THOUGHT. I GUESS WE SHOULD GO HOME.
WELL, MAYBE WE DON'T HAVE TO GO HOME JUST YET.

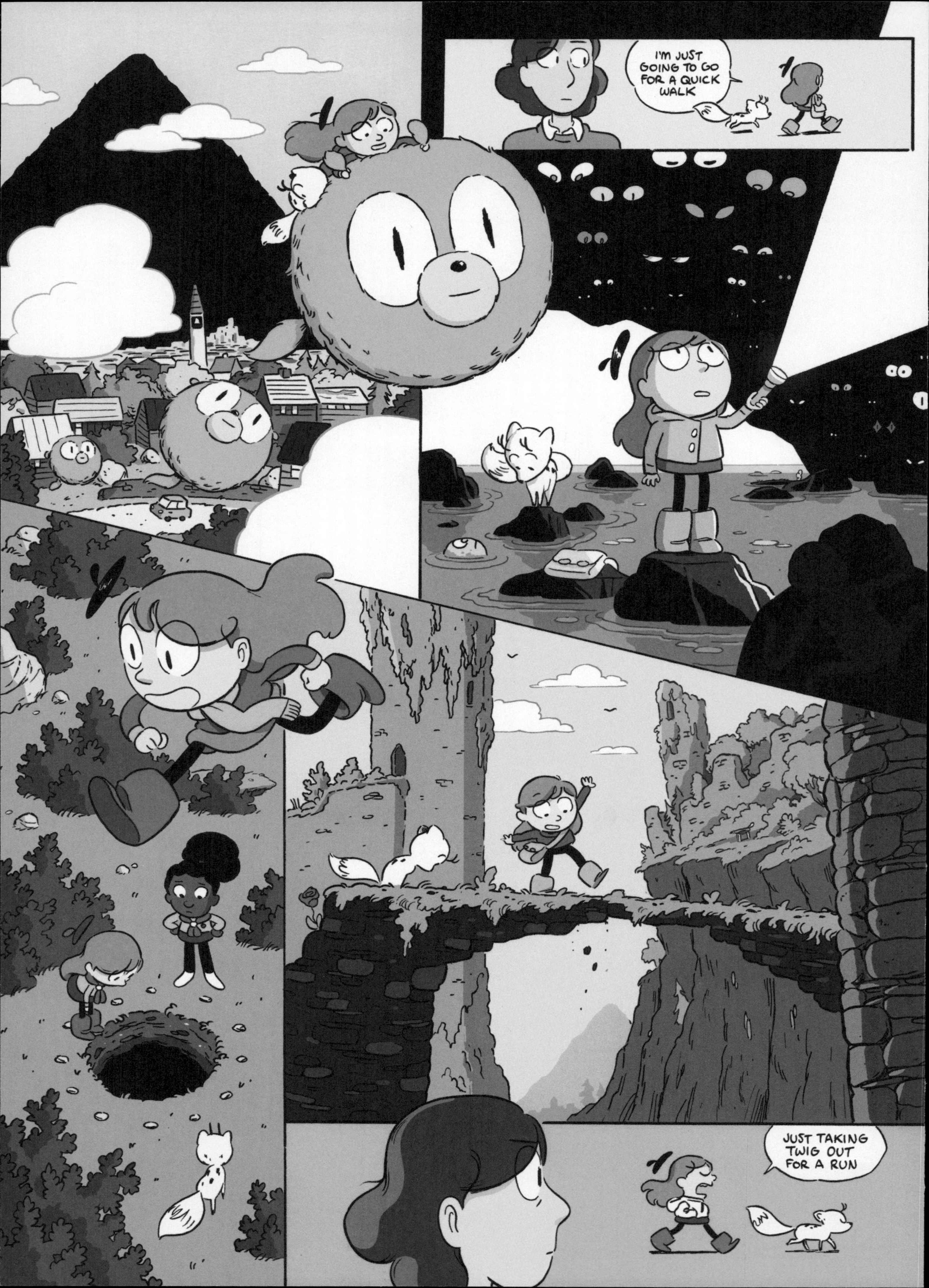
I'M JUST GOING TO GO FOR A QUICK WALK
JUST TAKING TWIG OUT FOR A RUN

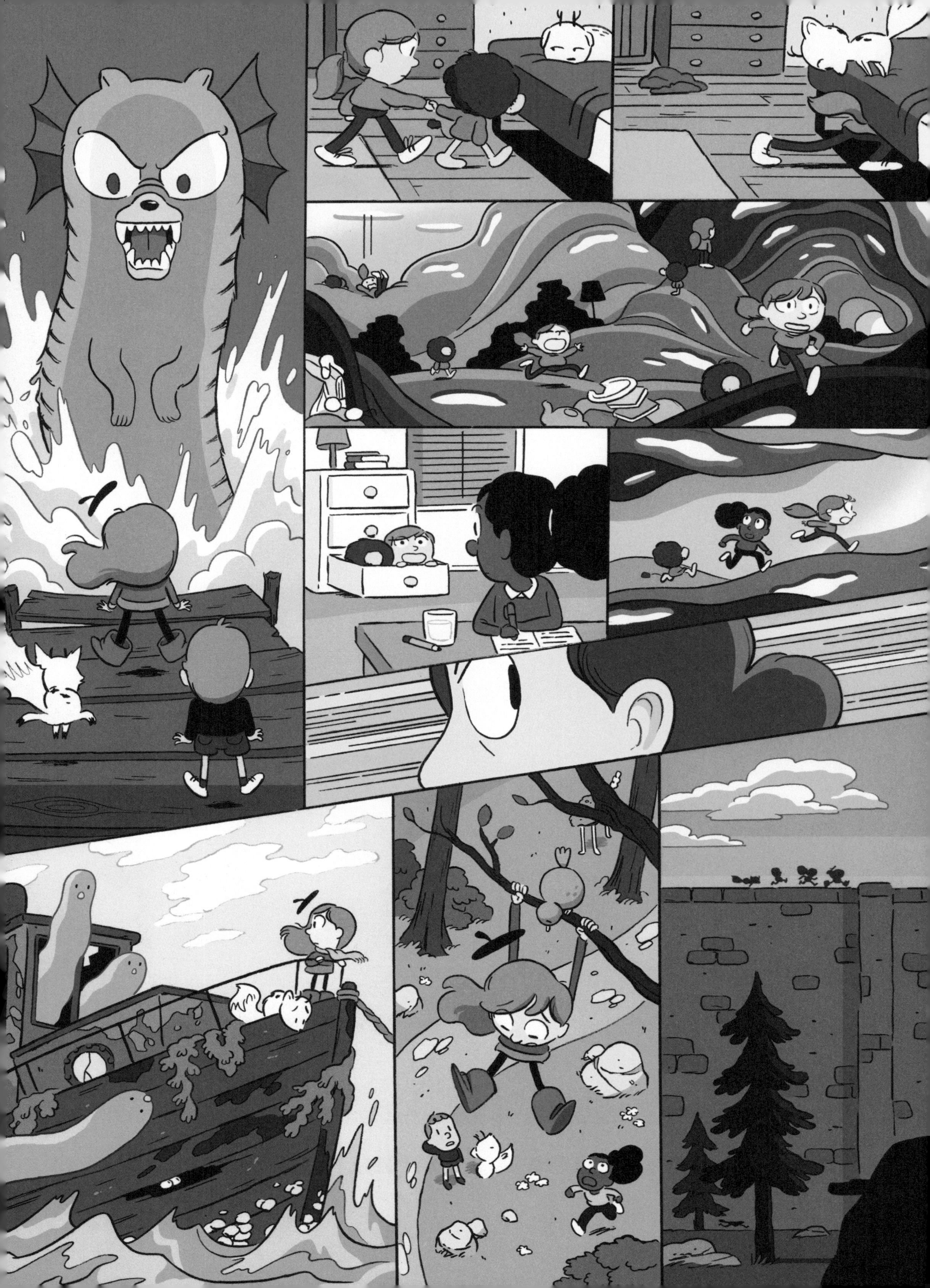

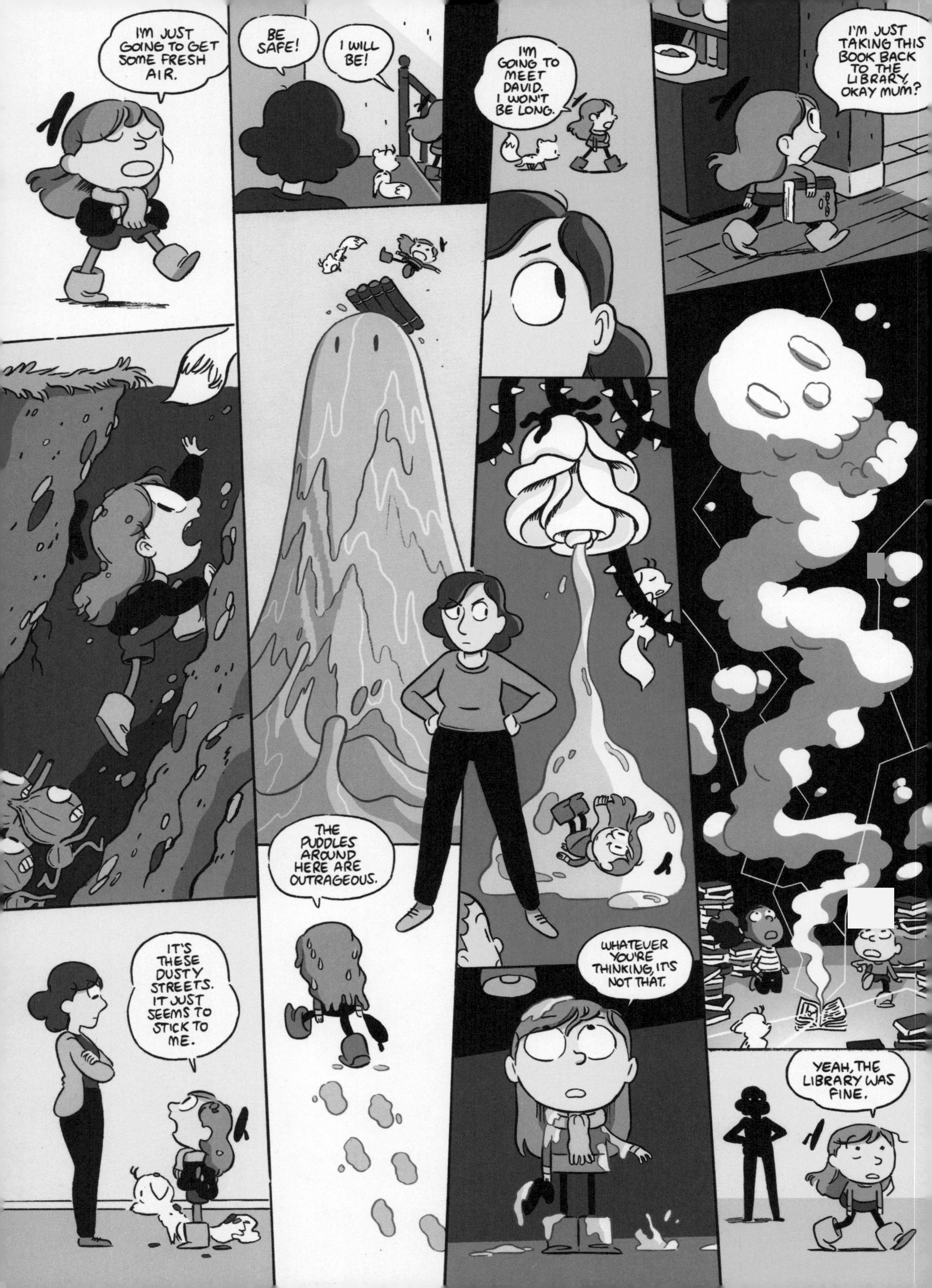

I'M JUST GOING TO GET SOME FRESH AIR.
BE SAFE!
I WILL BE!
I'M GOING TO MEET DAVID. I WON'T BE LONG.
I'M JUST TAKING THIS BOOK BACK TO THE LIBRARY, OKAY MUM?
THE PUDDLES AROUND HERE ARE OUTRAGEOUS.
IT'S THESE DUSTY STREETS. IT JUST SEEMS TO STICK TO ME.
WHATEVER YOU'RE THINKING, IT'S NOT THAT.
YEAH, THE LIBRARY WAS FINE.

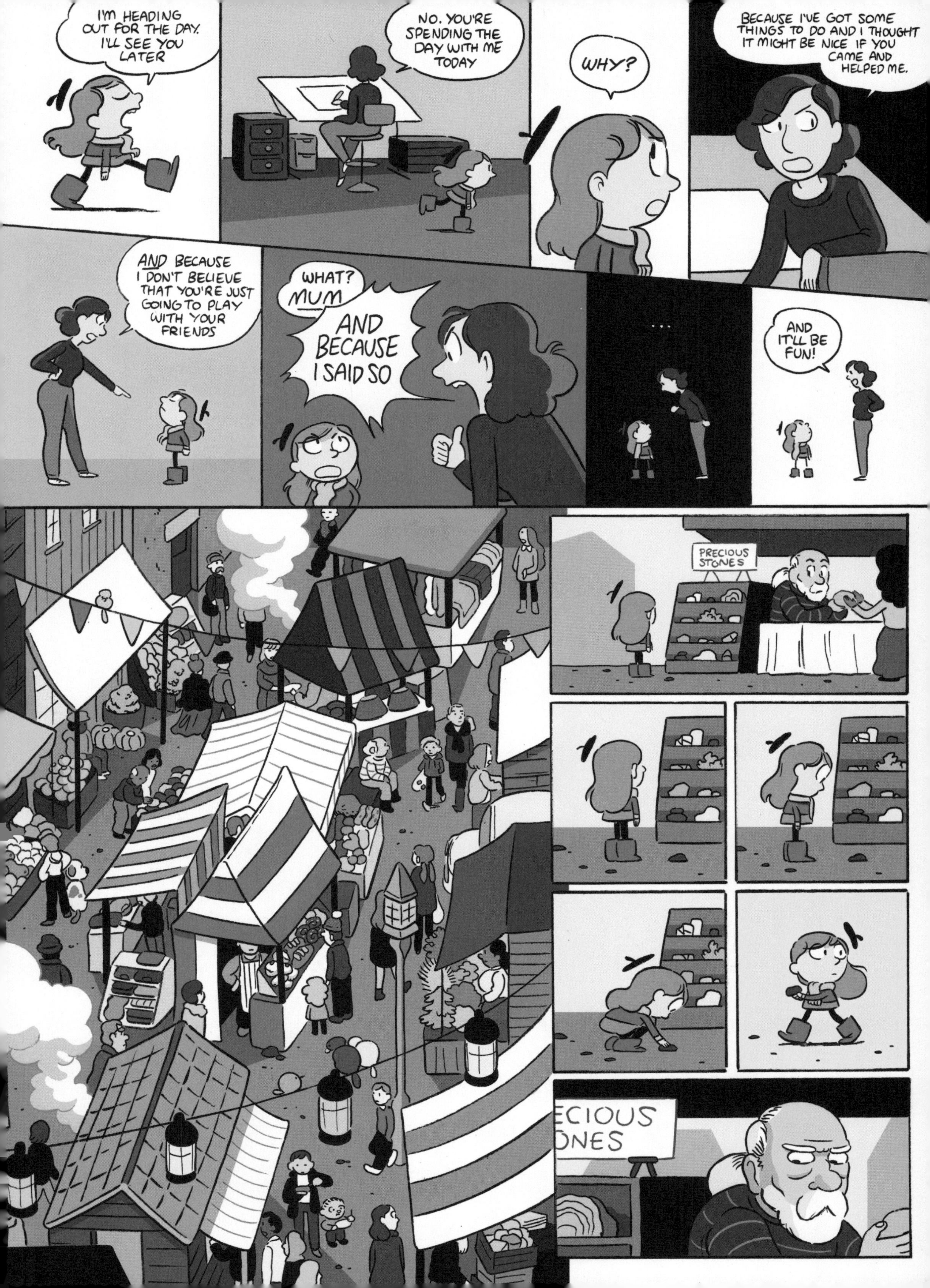

I'M HEADING OUT FOR THE DAY. I'LL SEE YOU LATER
NO. YOU'RE SPENDING THE DAY WITH ME TODAY
WHY?
BECAUSE I'VE GOT SOME THINGS TO DO AND I THOUGHT IT MIGHT BE NICE IF YOU CAME AND HELPED ME.
AND BECAUSE I DON'T BELIEVE THAT YOU'RE JUST GOING TO PLAY WITH YOUR FRIENDS
WHAT? MUM
AND BECAUSE I SAID SO
. . .
AND IT'LL BE FUN!
PRECIOUS STONES
ECIOUS
ONES

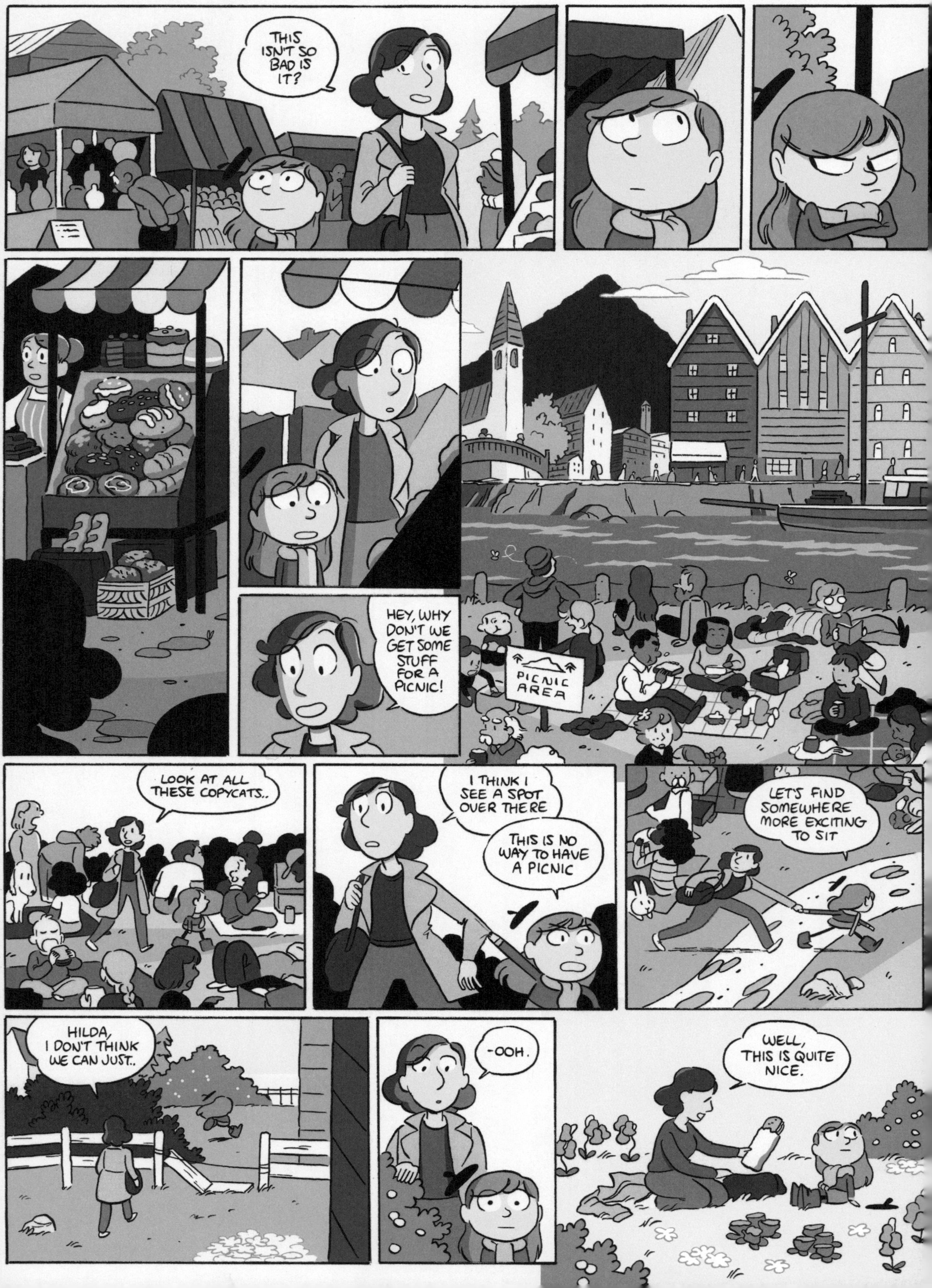
THIS ISN'T SO BAD IS IT?
HEY, WHY DON'T WE GET SOME STUFF FOR A PICNIC!
PICNIC AREA
LOOK AT ALL THESE COPYCATS..
I THINK I SEE A SPOT OVER THERE
THIS IS NO WAY TO HAVE A PICNIC
LET'S FIND SOMEWHERE MORE EXCITING TO SIT
HILDA, I DON'T THINK WE CAN JUST..
-OOH.
WELL, THIS IS QUITE NICE.

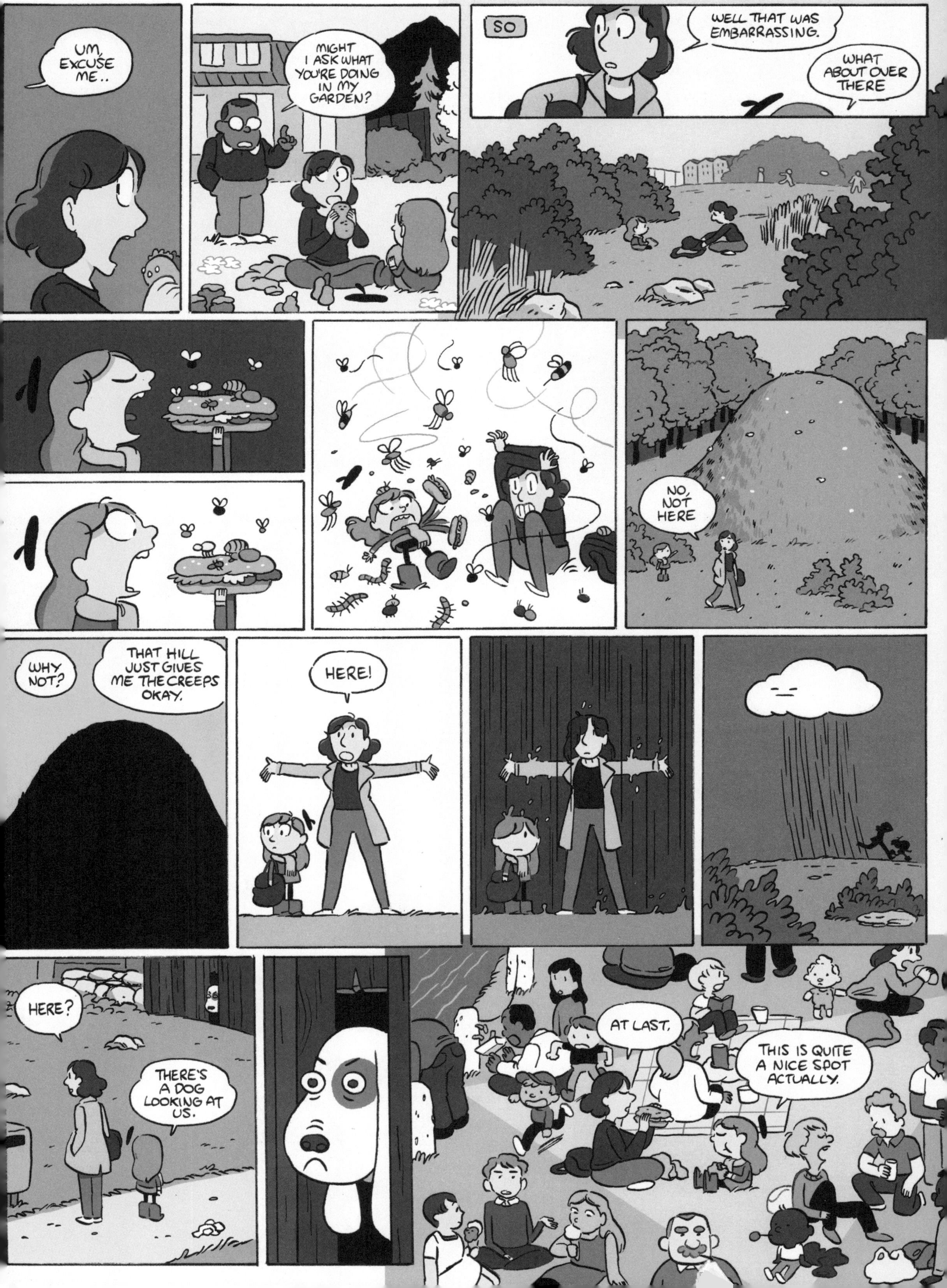
UM, EXCUSE ME..
MIGHT I ASK WHAT YOU'RE DOING IN MY GARDEN?
SO
WELL THAT WAS EMBARRASSING.
WHAT ABOUT OVER THERE
NO, NOT HERE
WHY NOT?
THAT HILL JUST GIVES ME THE CREEPS OKAY.
HERE!
HERE?
THERE'S A DOG LOOKING AT US.
AT LAST.
THIS IS QUITE A NICE SPOT ACTUALLY.

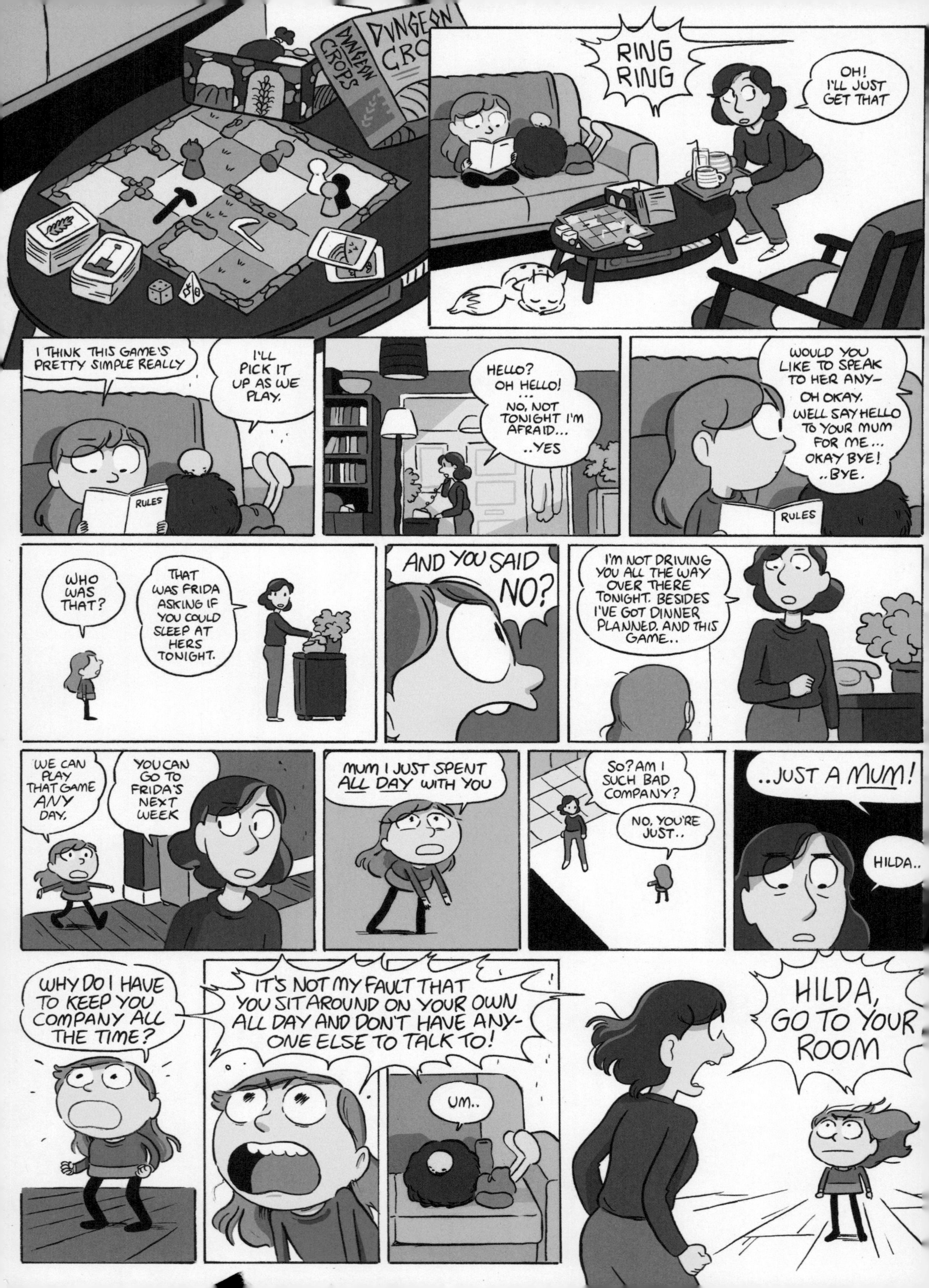
DUNGEON CROPS
RING RING
OH! I'LL JUST GET THAT
I THINK THIS GAME'S PRETTY SIMPLE REALLY
I'LL PICK IT UP AS WE PLAY.
RULES
HELLO? OH HELLO! ... NO, NOT TONIGHT I'M AFRAID... ..YES
WOULD YOU LIKE TO SPEAK TO HER ANY- OH OKAY. WELL SAY HELLO TO YOUR MUM FOR ME... OKAY BYE! ..BYE.
RULES
WHO WAS THAT?
THAT WAS FRIDA ASKING IF YOU COULD SLEEP AT HERS TONIGHT.
AND YOU SAID NO?
I'M NOT DRIVING YOU ALL THE WAY OVER THERE TONIGHT. BESIDES I'VE GOT DINNER PLANNED. AND THIS GAME..
WE CAN PLAY THAT GAME ANY DAY.
YOU CAN GO TO FRIDA'S NEXT WEEK
MUM I JUST SPENT ALL DAY WITH YOU
SO? AM I SUCH BAD COMPANY?
NO, YOU'RE JUST..
..JUST A MUM!
HILDA..
WHY DO I HAVE TO KEEP YOU COMPANY ALL THE TIME?
IT'S NOT MY FAULT THAT YOU SIT AROUND ON YOUR OWN ALL DAY AND DON'T HAVE ANY-ONE ELSE TO TALK TO!
UM..
HILDA, GO TO YOUR ROOM

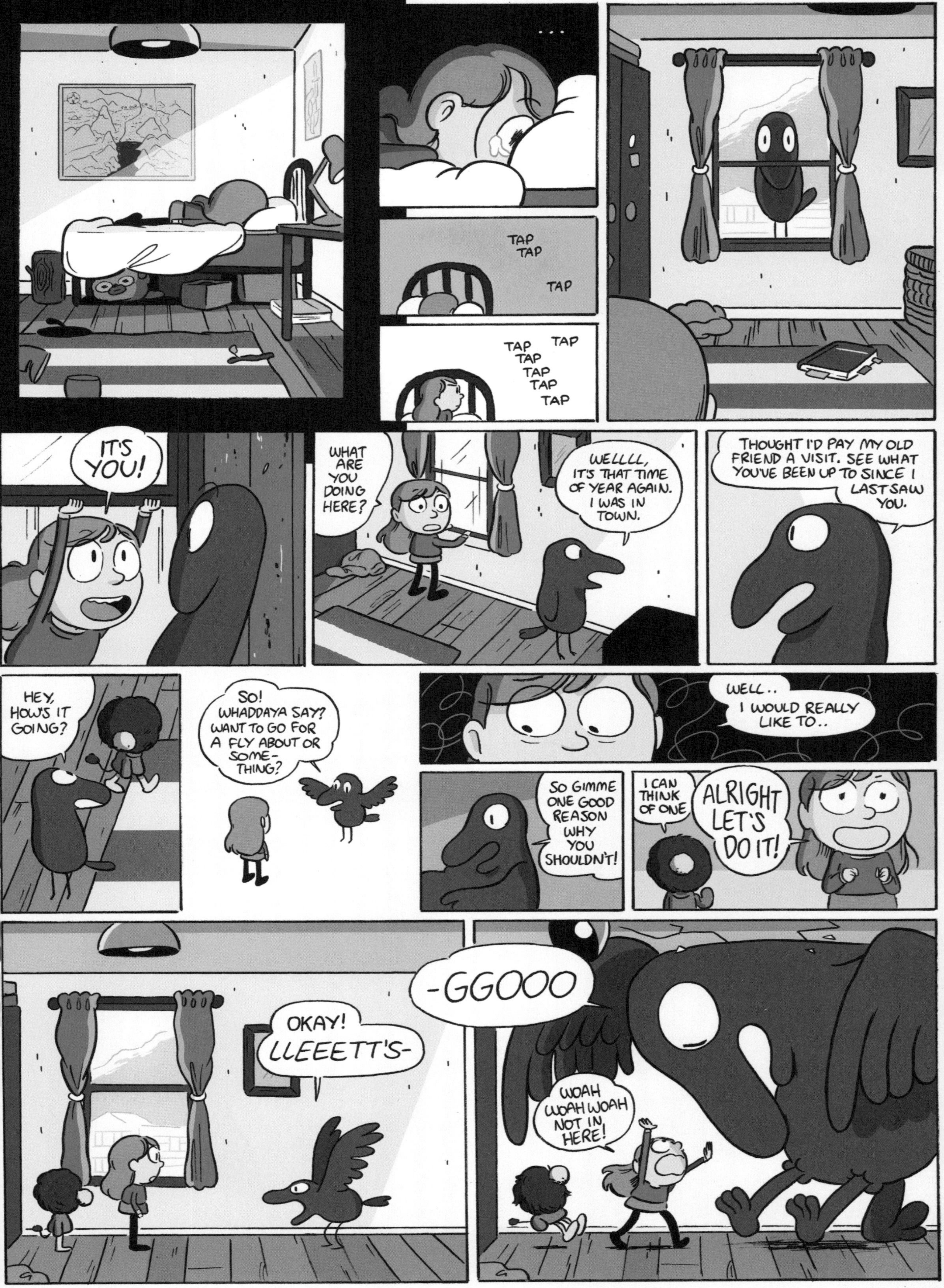
...
TAP
TAP
TAP
TAP TAP
TAP
TAP
TAP
TAP
IT'S YOU!
WHAT ARE YOU DOING HERE?
WELLLL, IT'S THAT TIME OF YEAR AGAIN. I WAS IN TOWN.
THOUGHT I'D PAY MY OLD FRIEND A VISIT. SEE WHAT YOU'VE BEEN UP TO SINCE I LAST SAW YOU.
HEY, HOW'S IT GOING?
SO! WHADDAYA SAY? WANT TO GO FOR A FLY ABOUT OR SOME-THING?
WELL.. I WOULD REALLY LIKE TO..
SO GIMME ONE GOOD REASON WHY YOU SHOULDN'T!
I CAN THINK OF ONE
ALRIGHT LET'S DO IT!
OKAY! LLEEETT'S-
-GGOOO
WOAH WOAH WOAH NOT IN HERE!

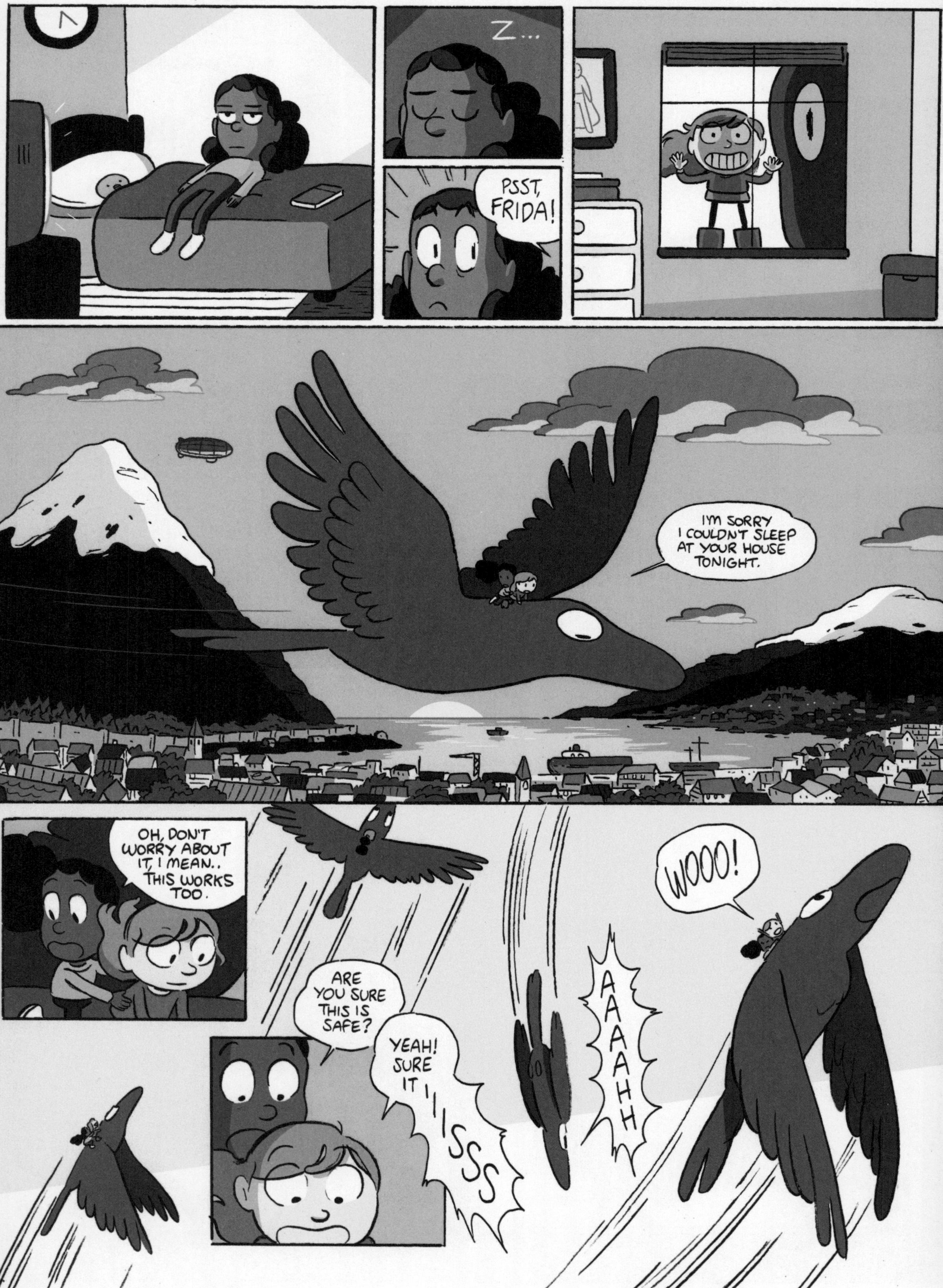
Z...
PSST, FRIDA!
I'M SORRY I COULDN'T SLEEP AT YOUR HOUSE TONIGHT.
OH, DON'T WORRY ABOUT IT, I MEAN.. THIS WORKS TOO.
ARE YOU SURE THIS IS SAFE?
YEAH! SURE IT IIISSSS
AAAAAHH
WOOO!

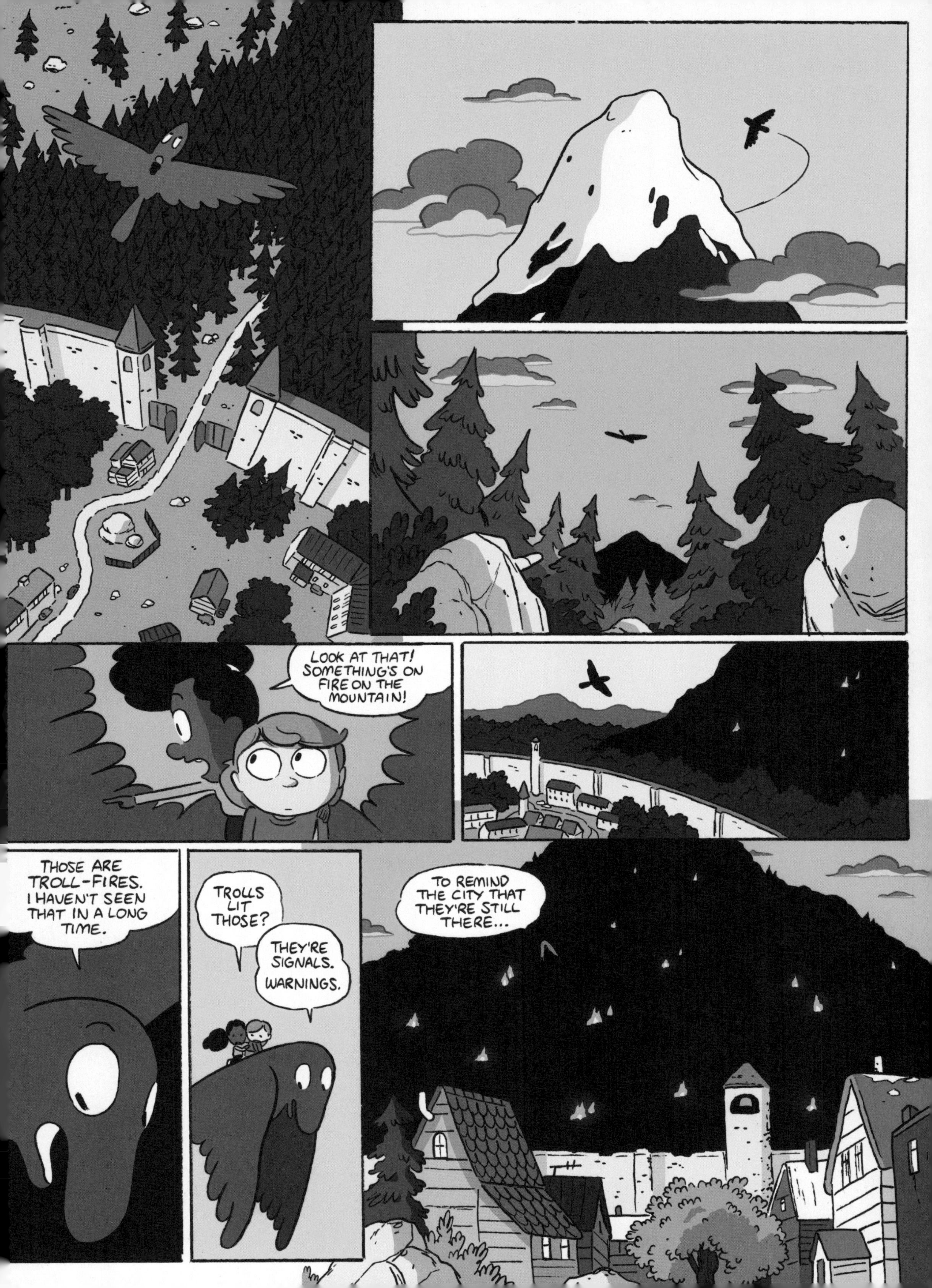
LOOK AT THAT! SOMETHING'S ON FIRE ON THE MOUNTAIN!
THOSE ARE TROLL-FIRES. I HAVEN'T SEEN THAT IN A LONG TIME.
TROLLS LIT THOSE?
THEY'RE SIGNALS. WARNINGS.
TO REMIND THE CITY THAT THEY'RE STILL THERE...

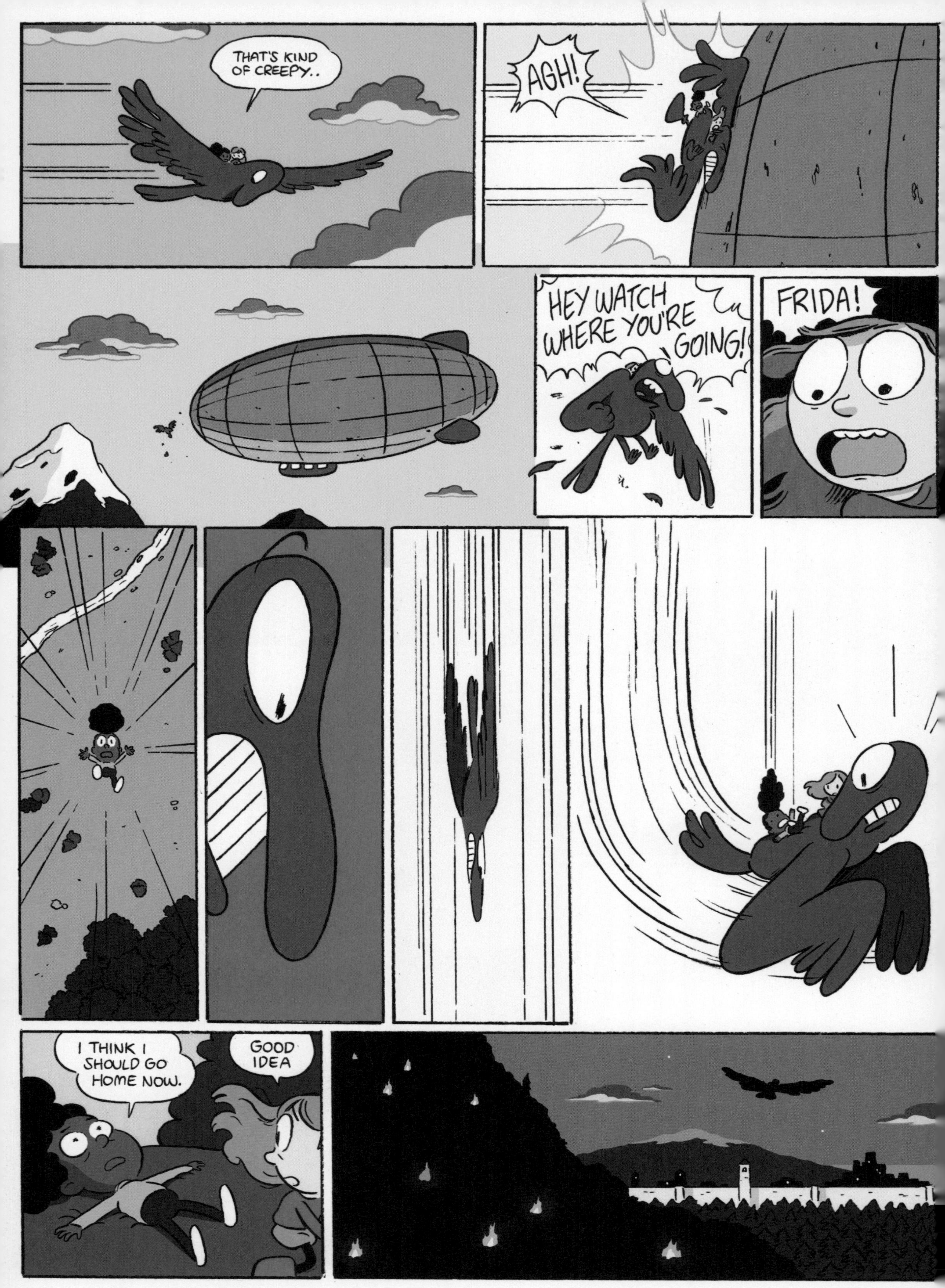
THAT'S KIND OF CREEPY..
AGH!
HEY WATCH WHERE YOU'RE GOING!
FRIDA!
I THINK I SHOULD GO HOME NOW.
GOOD IDEA

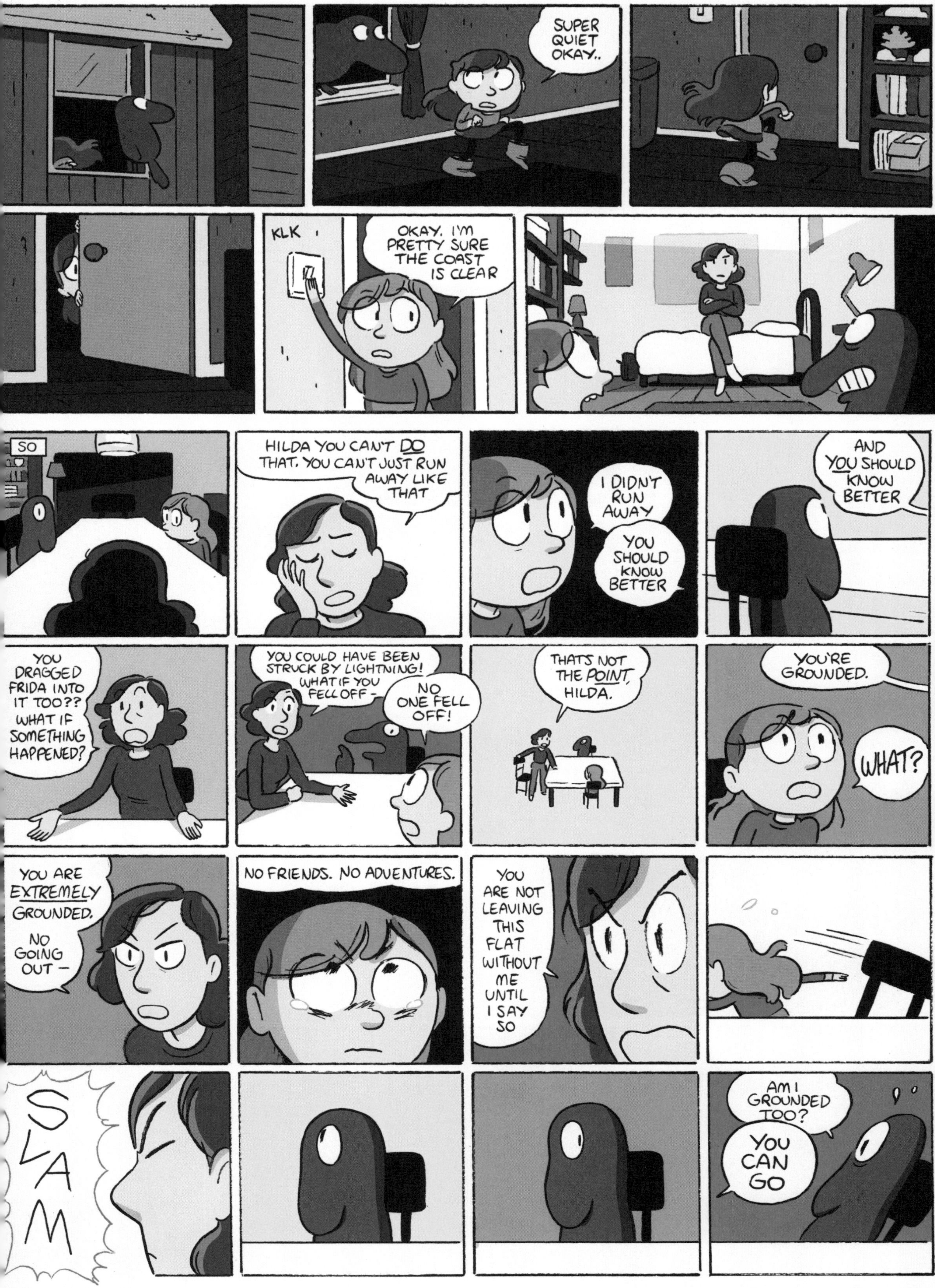
SUPER QUIET OKAY..
KLK
OKAY. I'M PRETTY SURE THE COAST IS CLEAR
SO
HILDA YOU CAN'T DO THAT. YOU CAN'T JUST RUN AWAY LIKE THAT
I DIDN'T RUN AWAY
YOU SHOULD KNOW BETTER
AND YOU SHOULD KNOW BETTER
YOU DRAGGED FRIDA INTO IT TOO?? WHAT IF SOMETHING HAPPENED?
YOU COULD HAVE BEEN STRUCK BY LIGHTNING! WHAT IF YOU FELL OFF -
NO ONE FELL OFF!
THATS NOT THE POINT, HILDA.
YOU'RE GROUNDED.
WHAT?
YOU ARE EXTREMELY GROUNDED.
NO GOING OUT -
NO FRIENDS. NO ADVENTURES.
YOU ARE NOT LEAVING THIS FLAT WITHOUT ME UNTIL I SAY SO
SLAM
AM I GROUNDED TOO?
YOU CAN GO

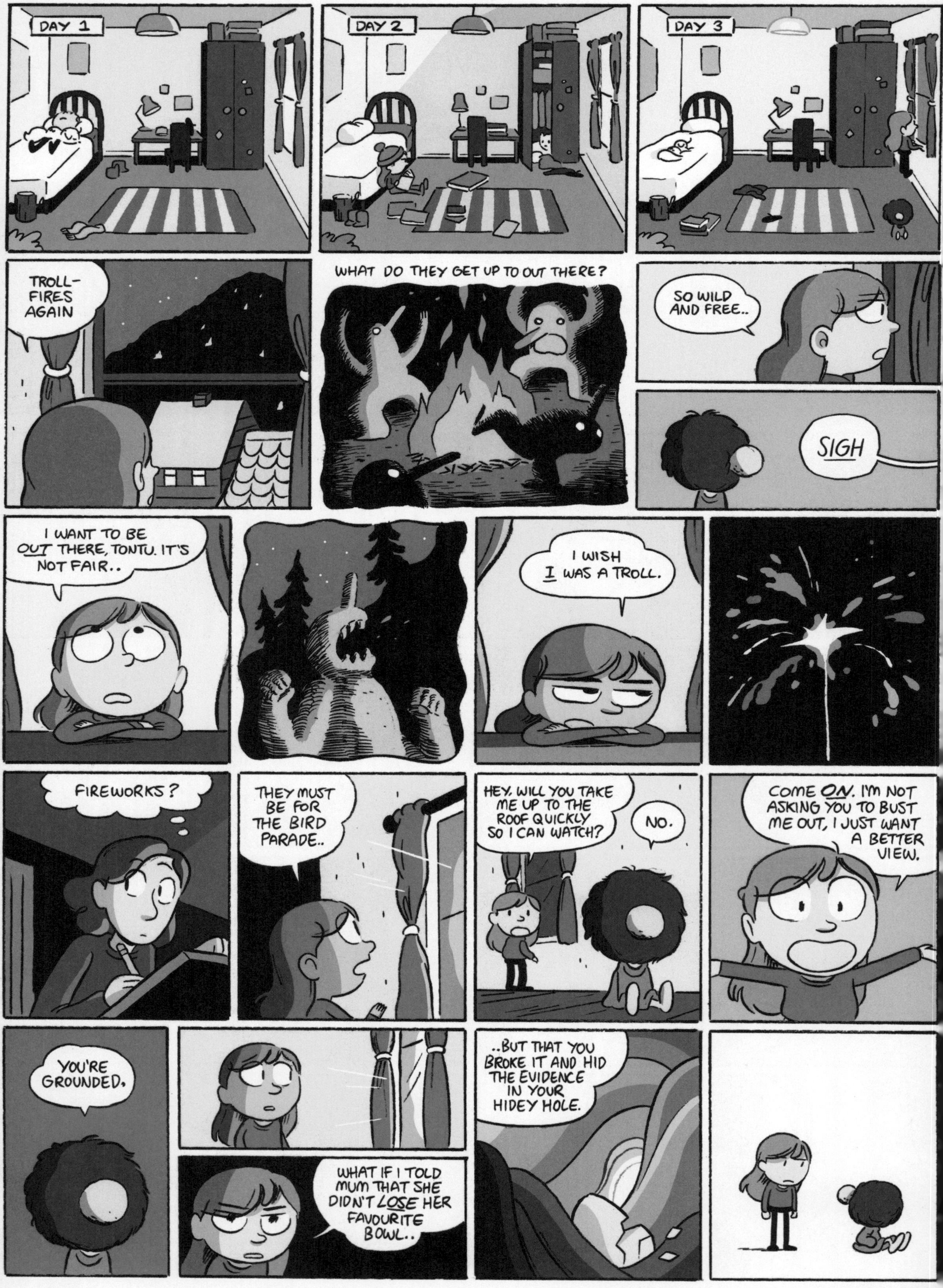

DAY 1
DAY 2
DAY 3
TROLL-FIRES AGAIN
WHAT DO THEY GET UP TO OUT THERE?
SO WILD AND FREE..
SIGH
I WANT TO BE OUT THERE, TONTU. IT'S NOT FAIR..
I WISH I WAS A TROLL.
FIREWORKS?
THEY MUST BE FOR THE BIRD PARADE..
HEY, WILL YOU TAKE ME UP TO THE ROOF QUICKLY SO I CAN WATCH?
NO.
COME ON. I'M NOT ASKING YOU TO BUST ME OUT, I JUST WANT A BETTER VIEW.
YOU'RE GROUNDED.
WHAT IF I TOLD MUM THAT SHE DIDN'T LOSE HER FAVOURITE BOWL..
..BUT THAT YOU BROKE IT AND HID THE EVIDENCE IN YOUR HIDEY HOLE.

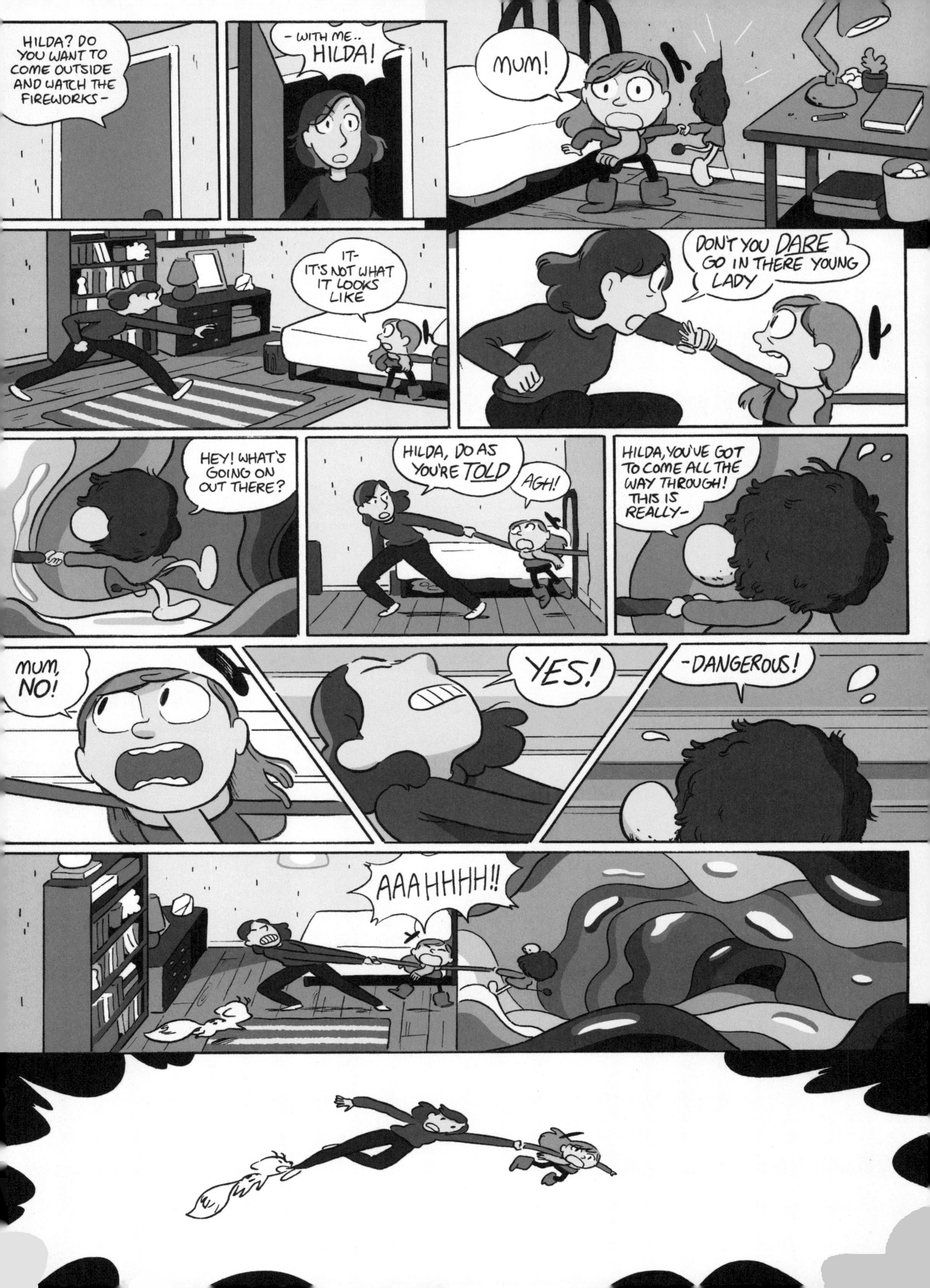
HILDA? DO YOU WANT TO COME OUTSIDE AND WATCH THE FIREWORKS -
- WITH ME.. HILDA!
MUM!
IT- IT'S NOT WHAT IT LOOKS LIKE
DON'T YOU DARE GO IN THERE YOUNG LADY
HEY! WHAT'S GOING ON OUT THERE?
HILDA, DO AS YOU'RE TOLD
AGH!
HILDA, YOU'VE GOT TO COME ALL THE WAY THROUGH! THIS IS REALLY-
MUM, NO!
YES!
-DANGEROUS!
AAAHHHH!!

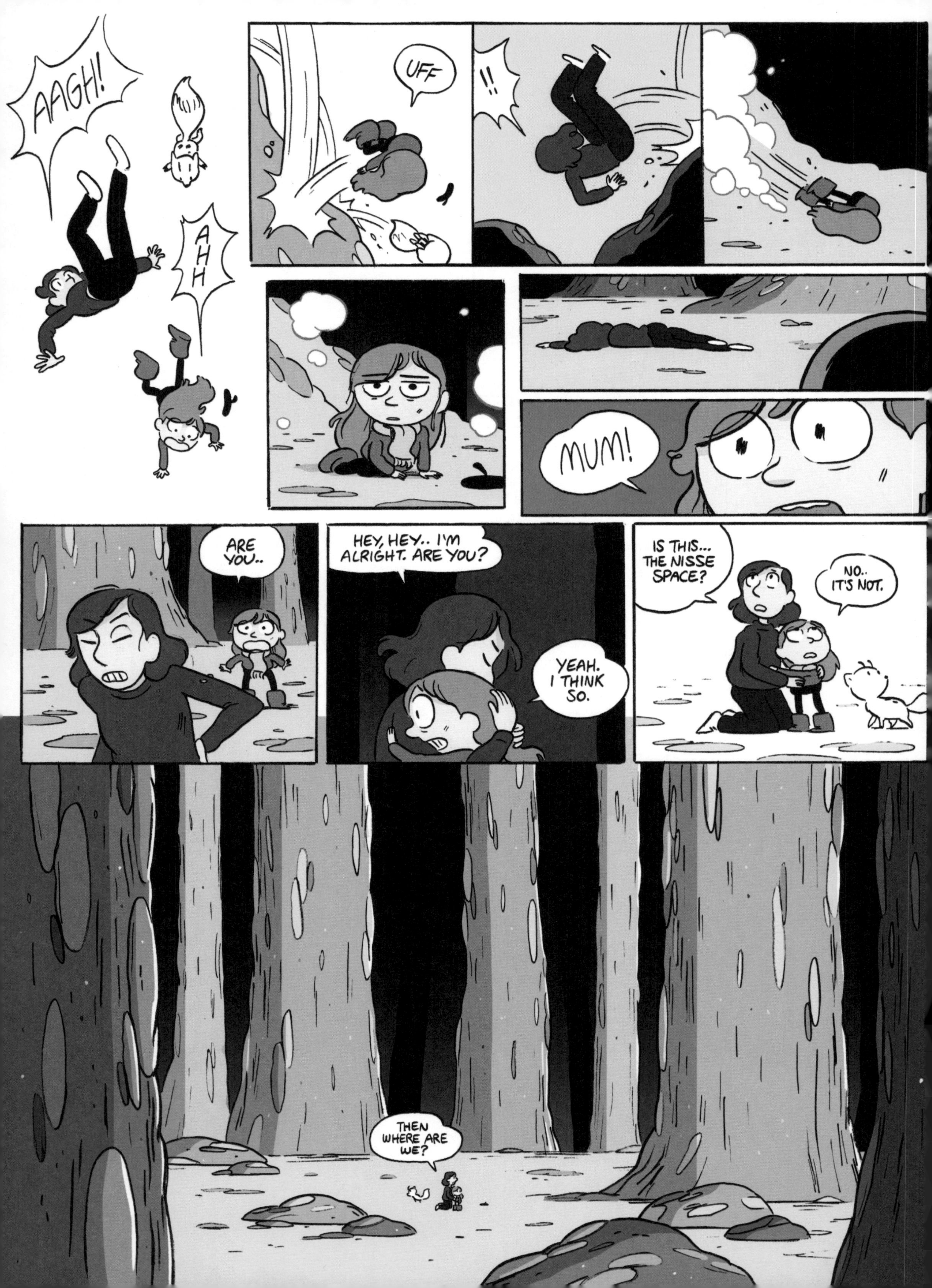

AAGH!
AHH
UFF
!!
MUM!
ARE YOU..
HEY, HEY.. I'M ALRIGHT. ARE YOU?
YEAH. I THINK SO.
IS THIS... THE NISSE SPACE?
NO.. IT'S NOT.
THEN WHERE ARE WE?

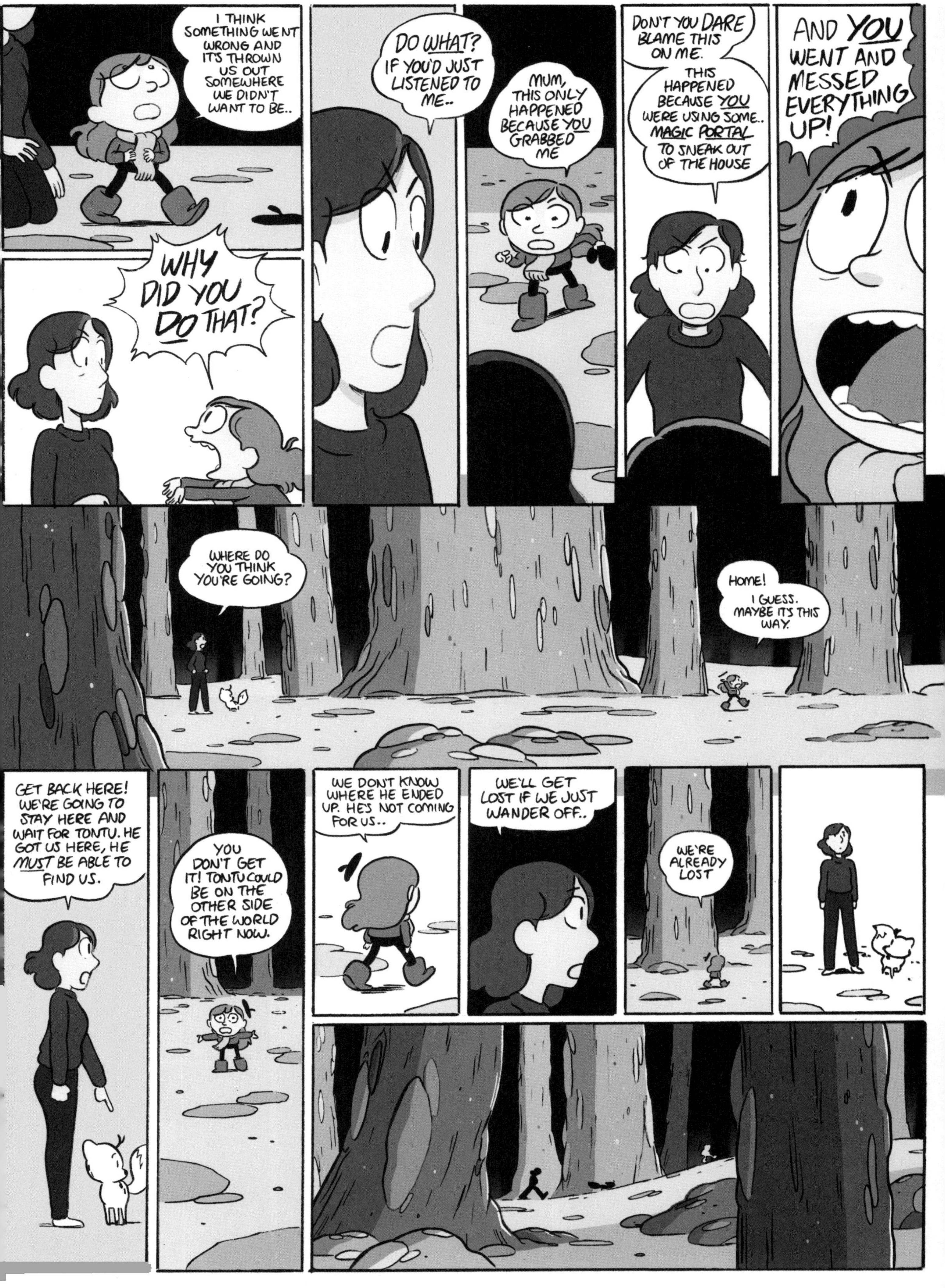
I THINK SOMETHING WENT WRONG AND IT'S THROWN US OUT SOMEWHERE WE DIDN'T WANT TO BE..
WHY DID YOU DO THAT?
DO WHAT? IF YOU'D JUST LISTENED TO ME..
MUM, THIS ONLY HAPPENED BECAUSE YOU GRABBED ME
DON'T YOU DARE BLAME THIS ON ME.
THIS HAPPENED BECAUSE YOU WERE USING SOME.. MAGIC PORTAL TO SNEAK OUT OF THE HOUSE
AND YOU WENT AND MESSED EVERYTHING UP!
WHERE DO YOU THINK YOU'RE GOING?
HOME! I GUESS. MAYBE IT'S THIS WAY.
GET BACK HERE! WE'RE GOING TO STAY HERE AND WAIT FOR TONTU. HE GOT US HERE, HE MUST BE ABLE TO FIND US.
YOU DON'T GET IT! TONTU COULD BE ON THE OTHER SIDE OF THE WORLD RIGHT NOW.
WE DON'T KNOW WHERE HE ENDED UP. HE'S NOT COMING FOR US..
WE'LL GET LOST IF WE JUST WANDER OFF..
WE'RE ALREADY LOST

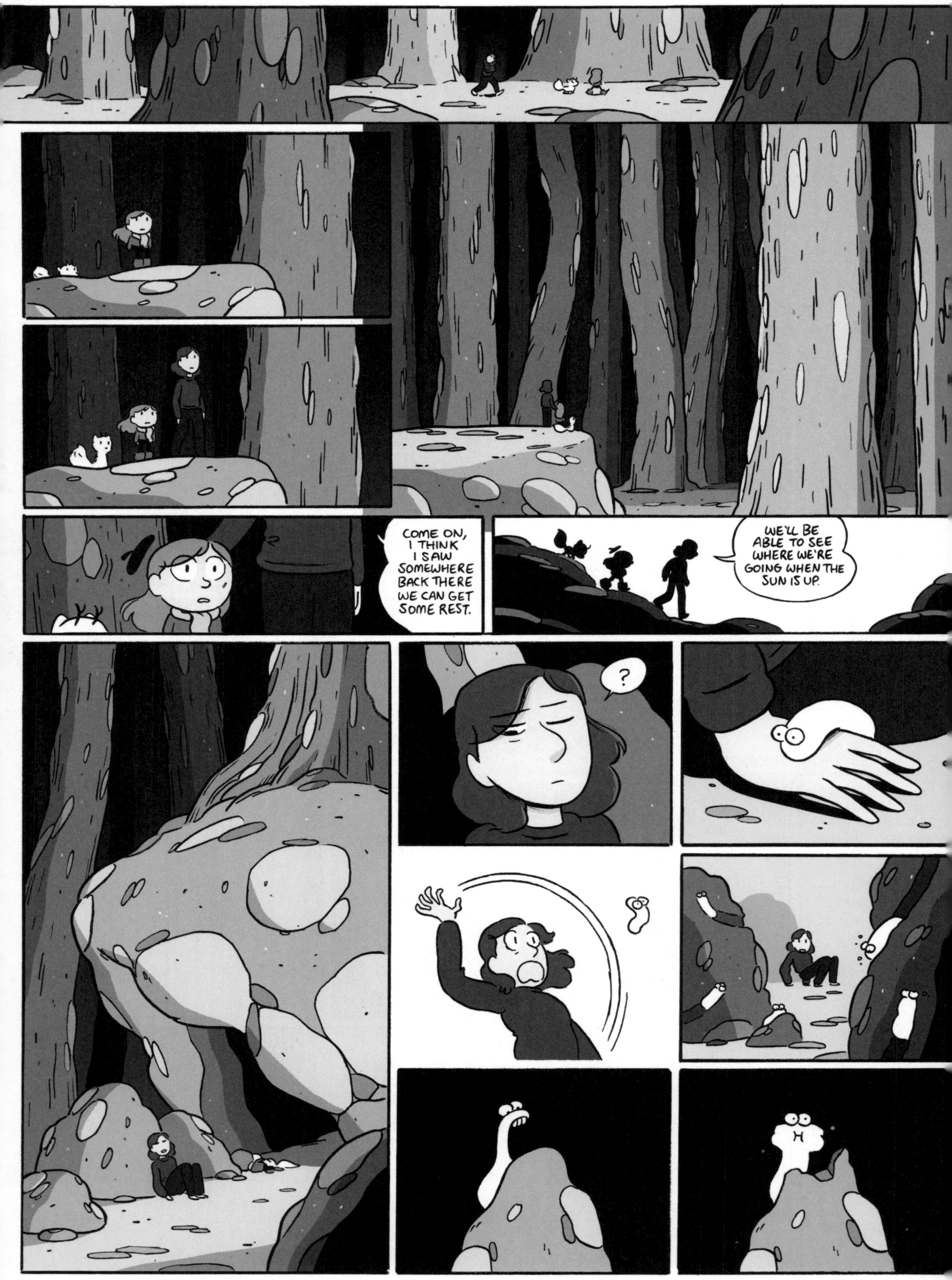
COME ON, I THINK I SAW SOMEWHERE BACK THERE WE CAN GET SOME REST.
WE'LL BE ABLE TO SEE WHERE WE'RE GOING WHEN THE SUN IS UP.
?

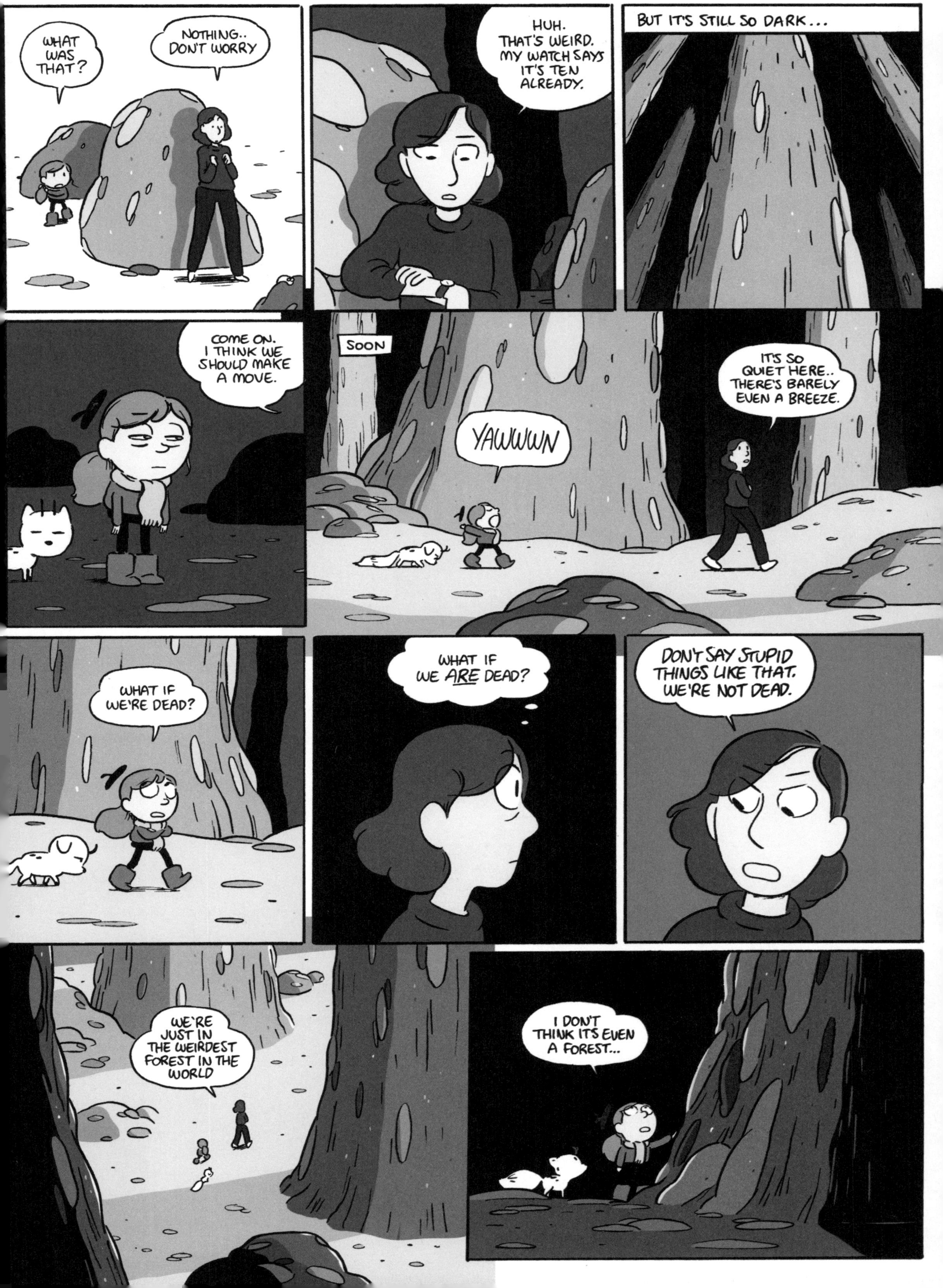
WHAT WAS THAT?
NOTHING.. DON'T WORRY
HUH. THAT'S WEIRD. MY WATCH SAYS IT'S TEN ALREADY.
BUT IT'S STILL SO DARK...
COME ON. I THINK WE SHOULD MAKE A MOVE.
SOON
IT'S SO QUIET HERE.. THERE'S BARELY EVEN A BREEZE.
YAWWWN
WHAT IF WE'RE DEAD?
WHAT IF WE ARE DEAD?
DON'T SAY STUPID THINGS LIKE THAT. WE'RE NOT DEAD.
WE'RE JUST IN THE WEIRDEST FOREST IN THE WORLD
I DON'T THINK IT'S EVEN A FOREST...

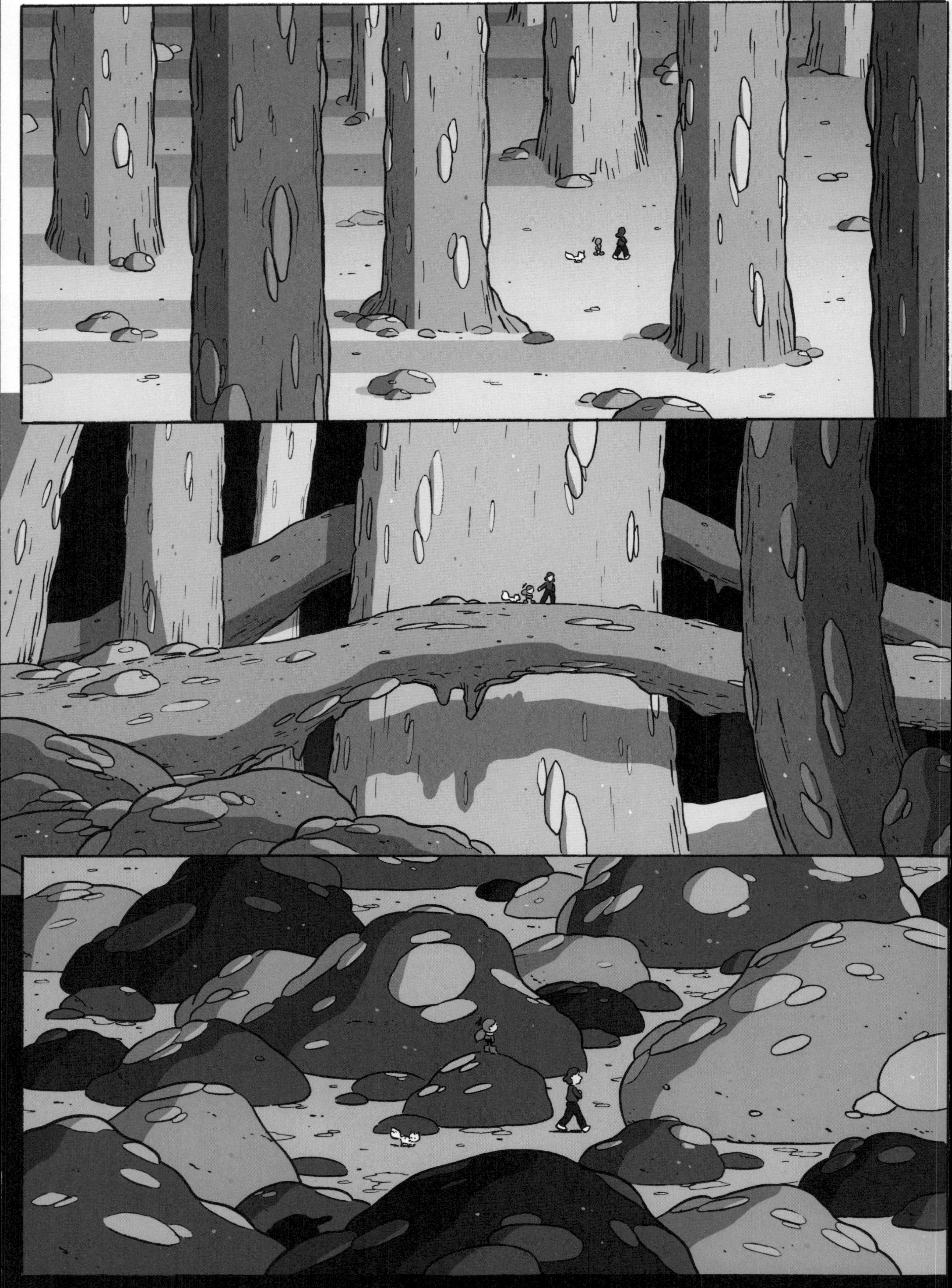

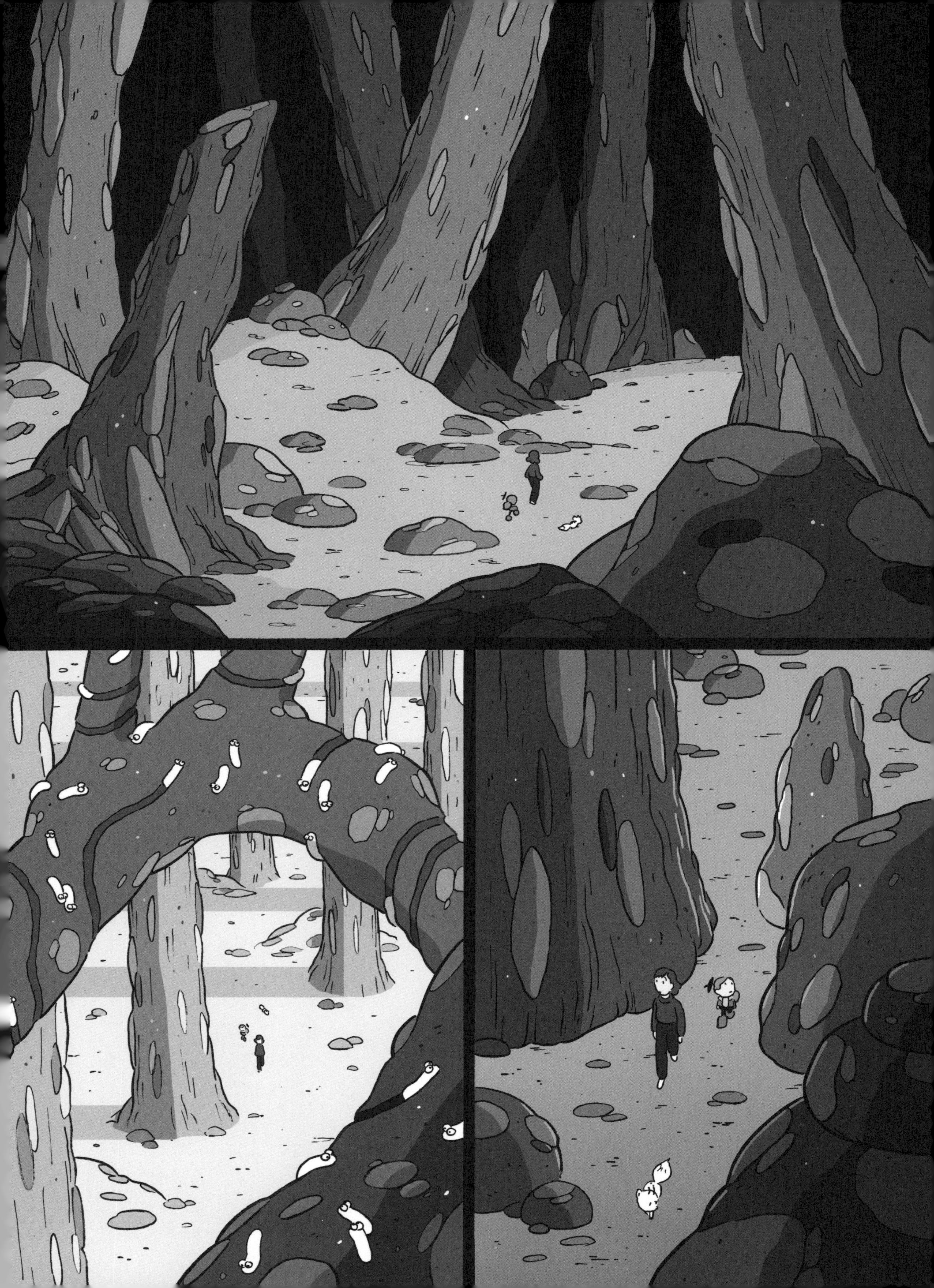

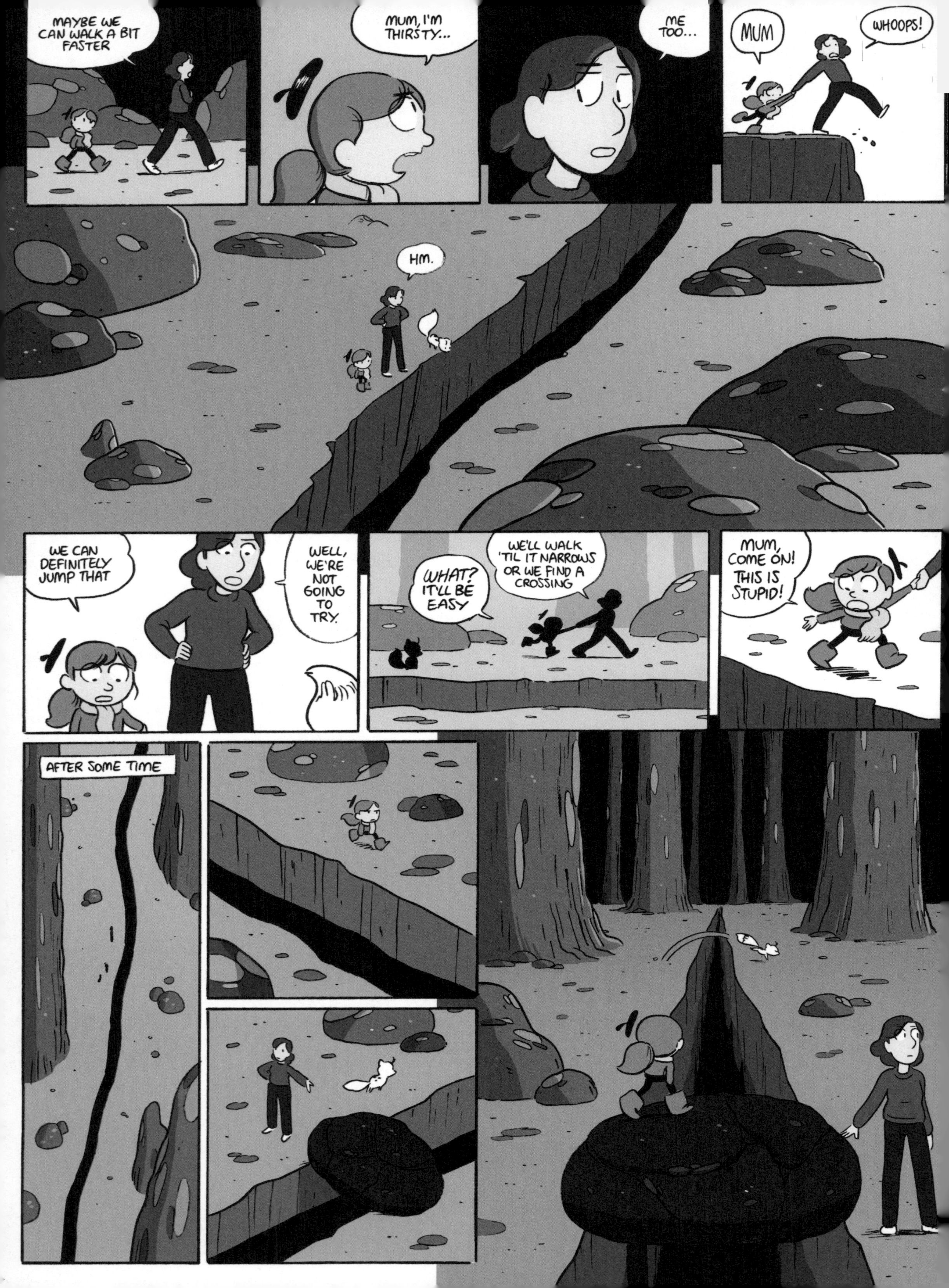

MAYBE WE CAN WALK A BIT FASTER
MUM, I'M THIRSTY...
ME TOO...
MUM
WHOOPS!
HM.
WE CAN DEFINITELY JUMP THAT
WELL, WE'RE NOT GOING TO TRY.
WHAT? IT'LL BE EASY
WE'LL WALK 'TIL IT NARROWS OR WE FIND A CROSSING
MUM, COME ON! THIS IS STUPID!
AFTER SOME TIME

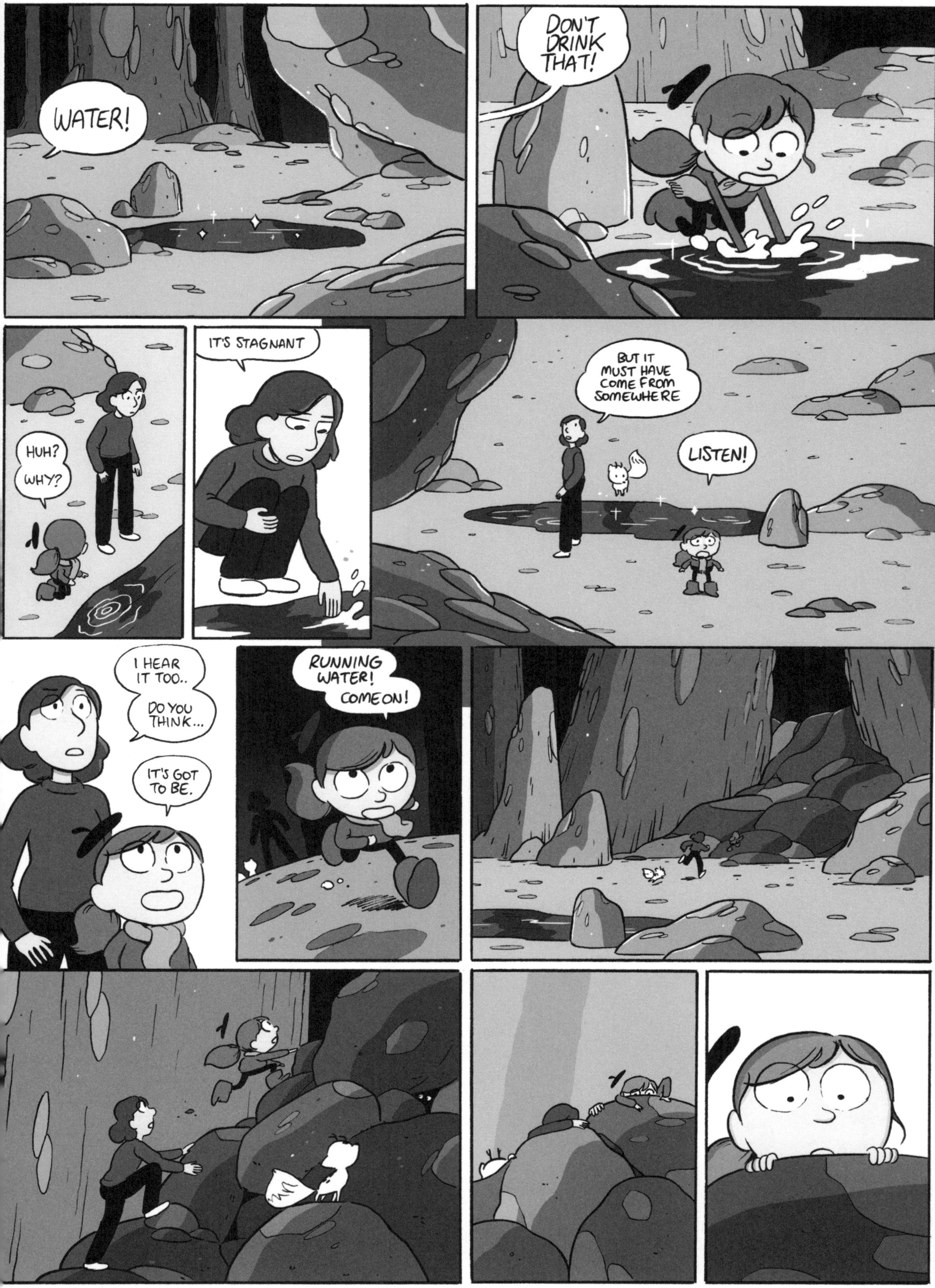
WATER!
DON'T DRINK THAT!
HUH?
WHY?
IT'S STAGNANT
BUT IT MUST HAVE COME FROM SOMEWHERE
LISTEN!
I HEAR IT TOO..
DO YOU THINK...
IT'S GOT TO BE.
RUNNING WATER!
COME ON!

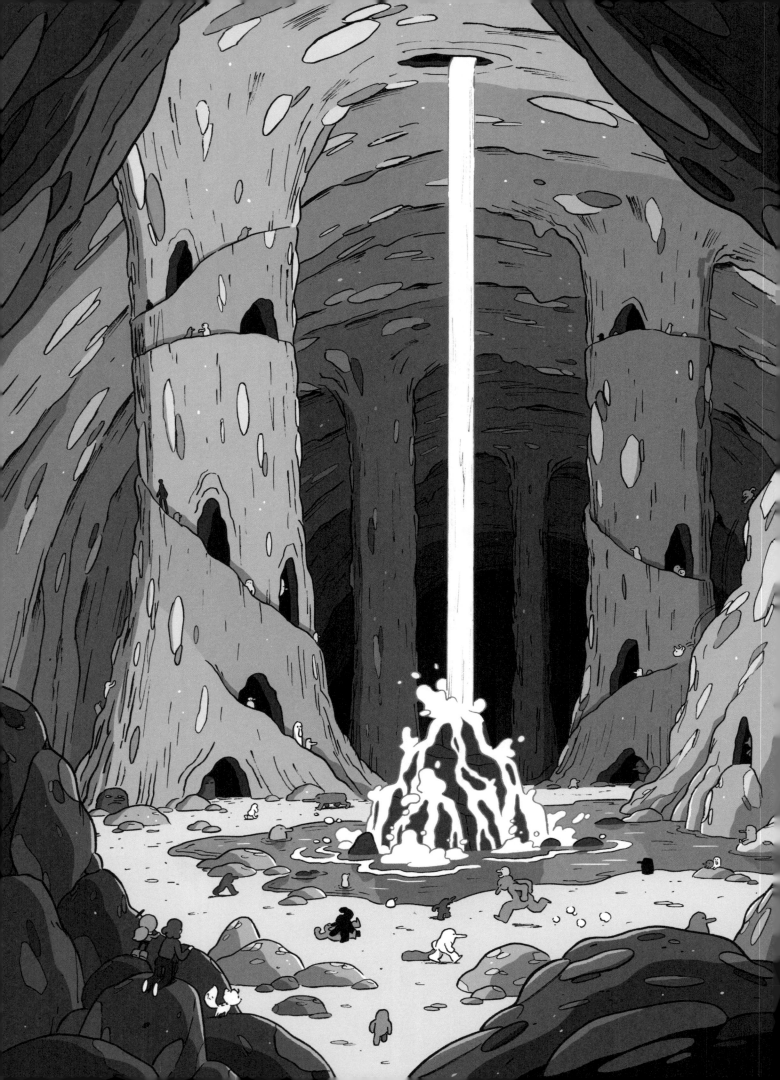

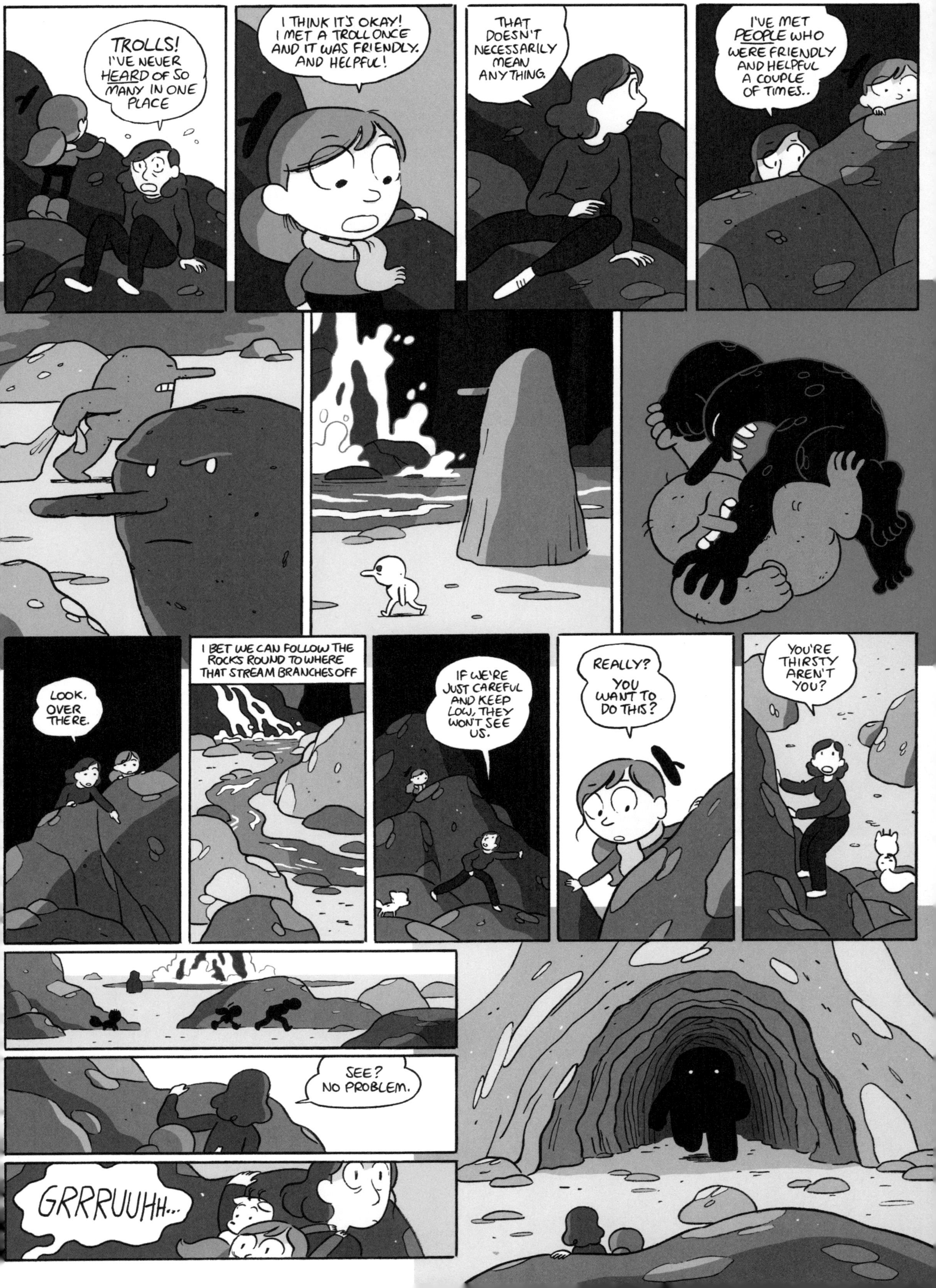
TROLLS! I'VE NEVER HEARD OF SO MANY IN ONE PLACE
I THINK IT'S OKAY! I MET A TROLL ONCE AND IT WAS FRIENDLY. AND HELPFUL!
THAT DOESN'T NECESSARILY MEAN ANYTHING.
I'VE MET PEOPLE WHO WERE FRIENDLY AND HELPFUL A COUPLE OF TIMES..
LOOK. OVER THERE.
I BET WE CAN FOLLOW THE ROCKS ROUND TO WHERE THAT STREAM BRANCHES OFF
IF WE'RE JUST CAREFUL AND KEEP LOW, THEY WON'T SEE US.
REALLY? YOU WANT TO DO THIS?
YOU'RE THIRSTY AREN'T YOU?
SEE? NO PROBLEM.
GRRRUUHH...

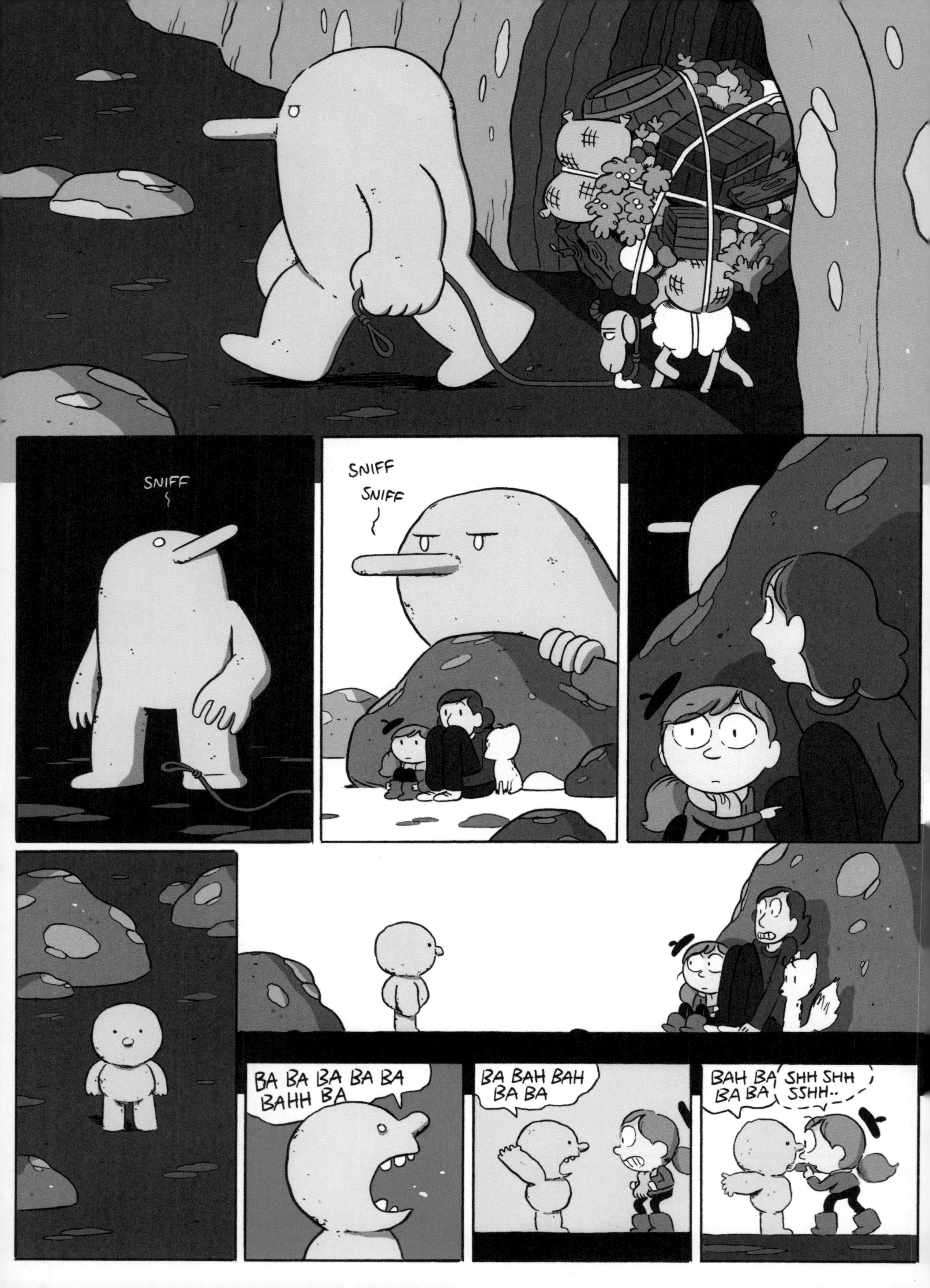
SNIFF
SNIFF
SNIFF
BA BA BA BA BA BAHH BA
BA BAH BAH BA BA
BAH BA BA BA
SHH SHH SSHH..

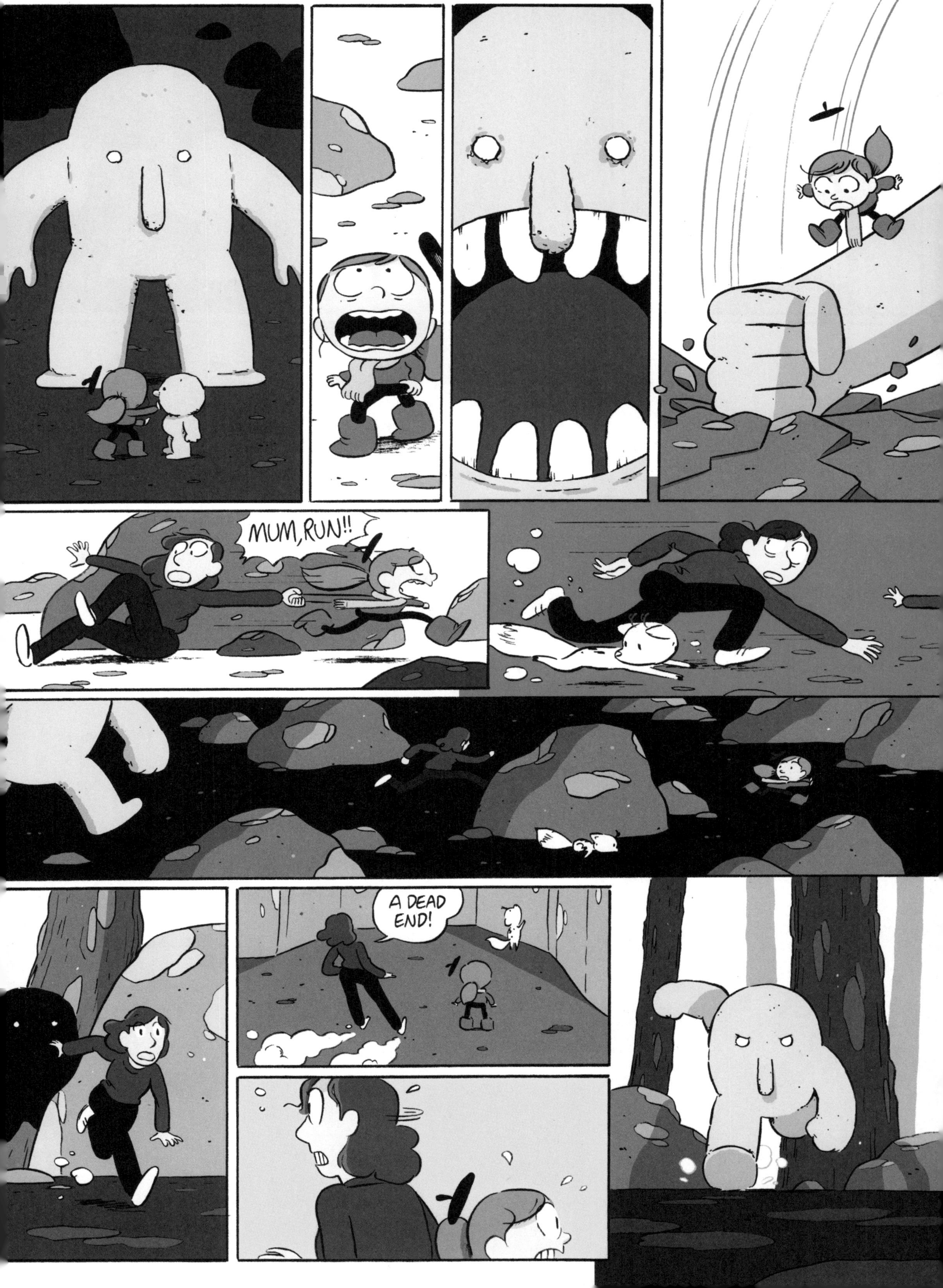
MUM, RUN!!
A DEAD END!

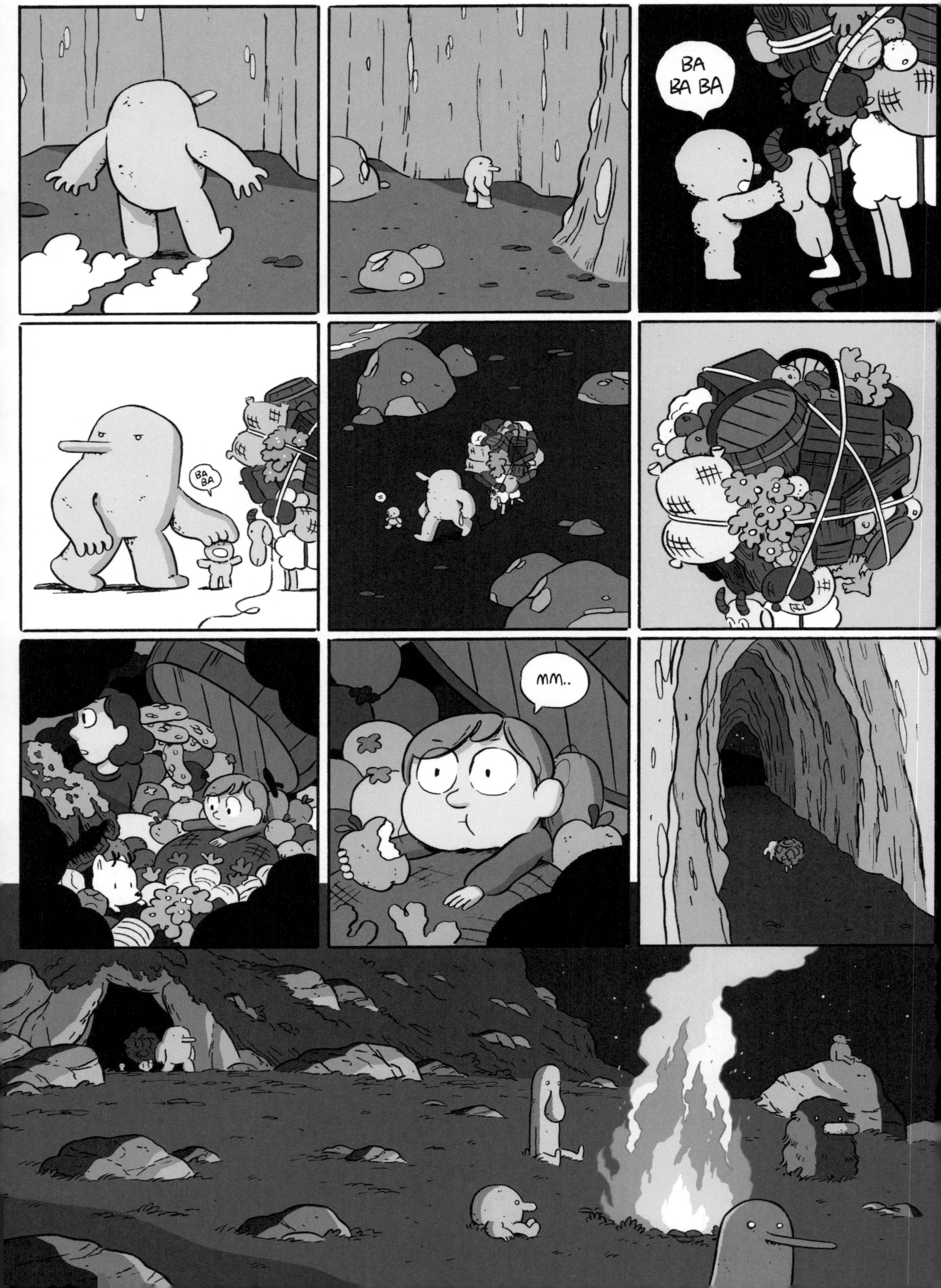
BA
BA BA
BA
BA
MM..

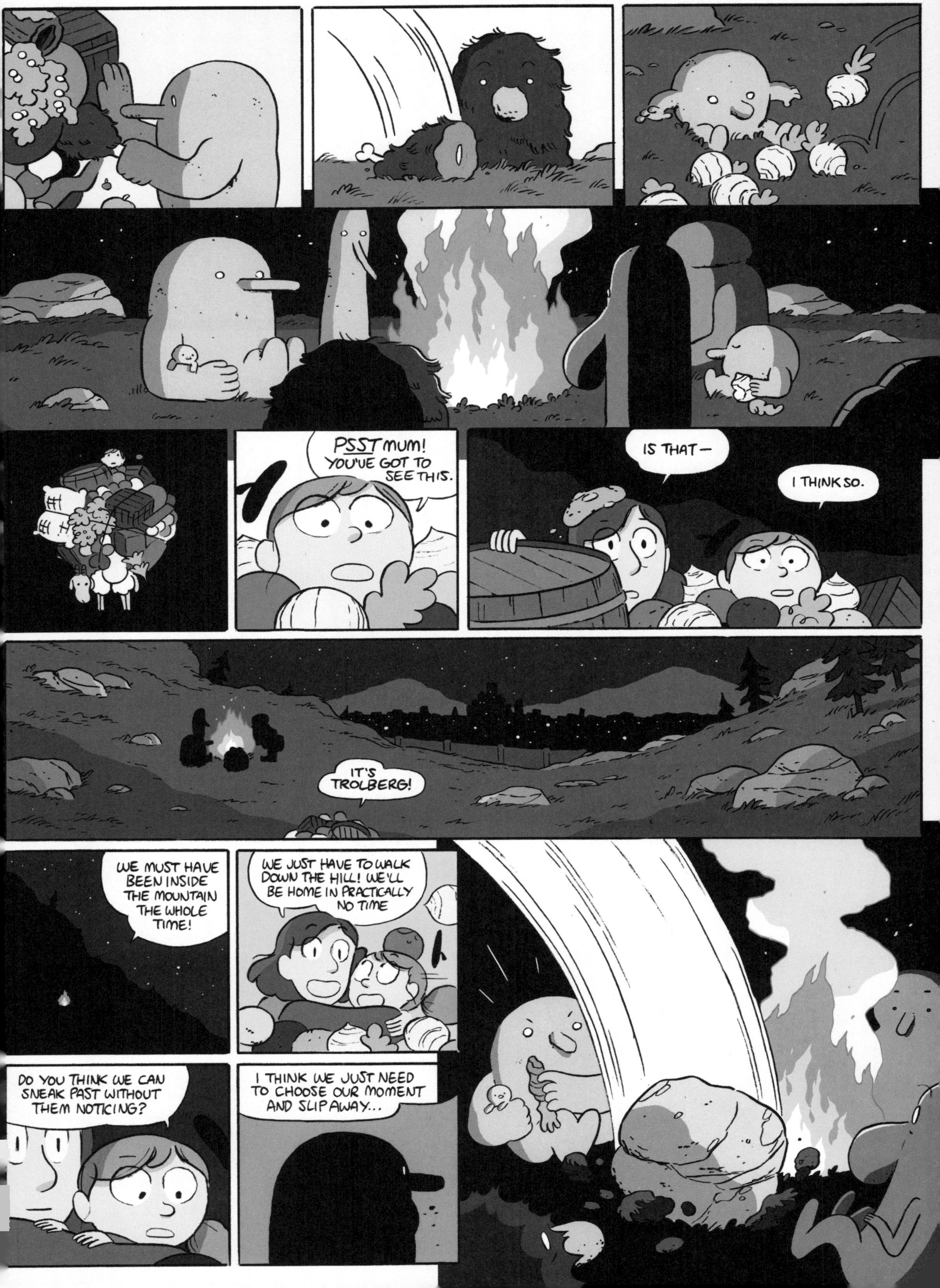
PSST MUM! YOU'VE GOT TO SEE THIS.
IS THAT—
I THINK SO.
IT'S TROLBERG!
WE MUST HAVE BEEN INSIDE THE MOUNTAIN THE WHOLE TIME!
WE JUST HAVE TO WALK DOWN THE HILL! WE'LL BE HOME IN PRACTICALLY NO TIME
DO YOU THINK WE CAN SNEAK PAST WITHOUT THEM NOTICING?
I THINK WE JUST NEED TO CHOOSE OUR MOMENT AND SLIP AWAY...

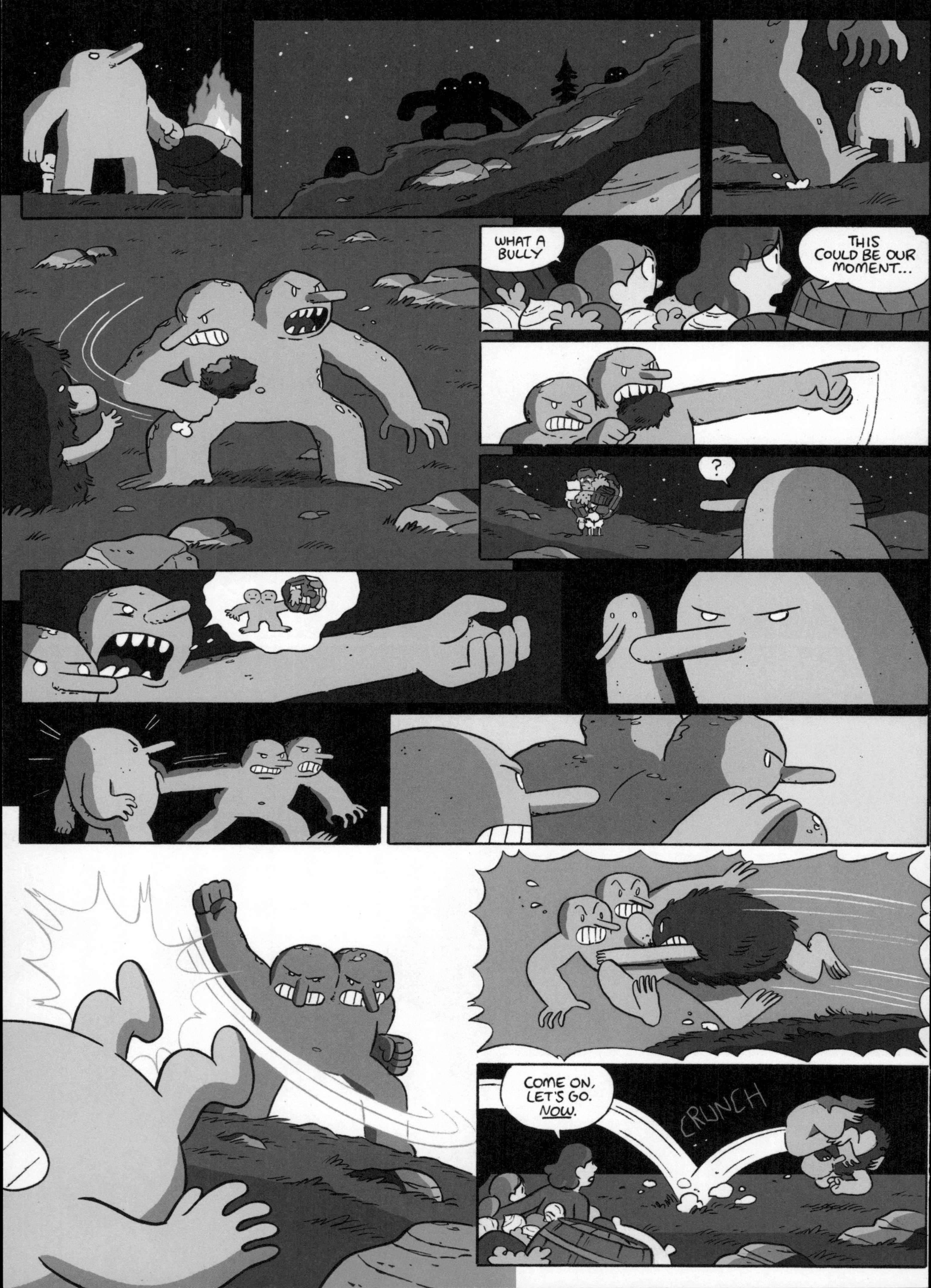
WHAT A BULLY
THIS COULD BE OUR MOMENT...
?
COME ON, LET'S GO. NOW.
CRUNCH

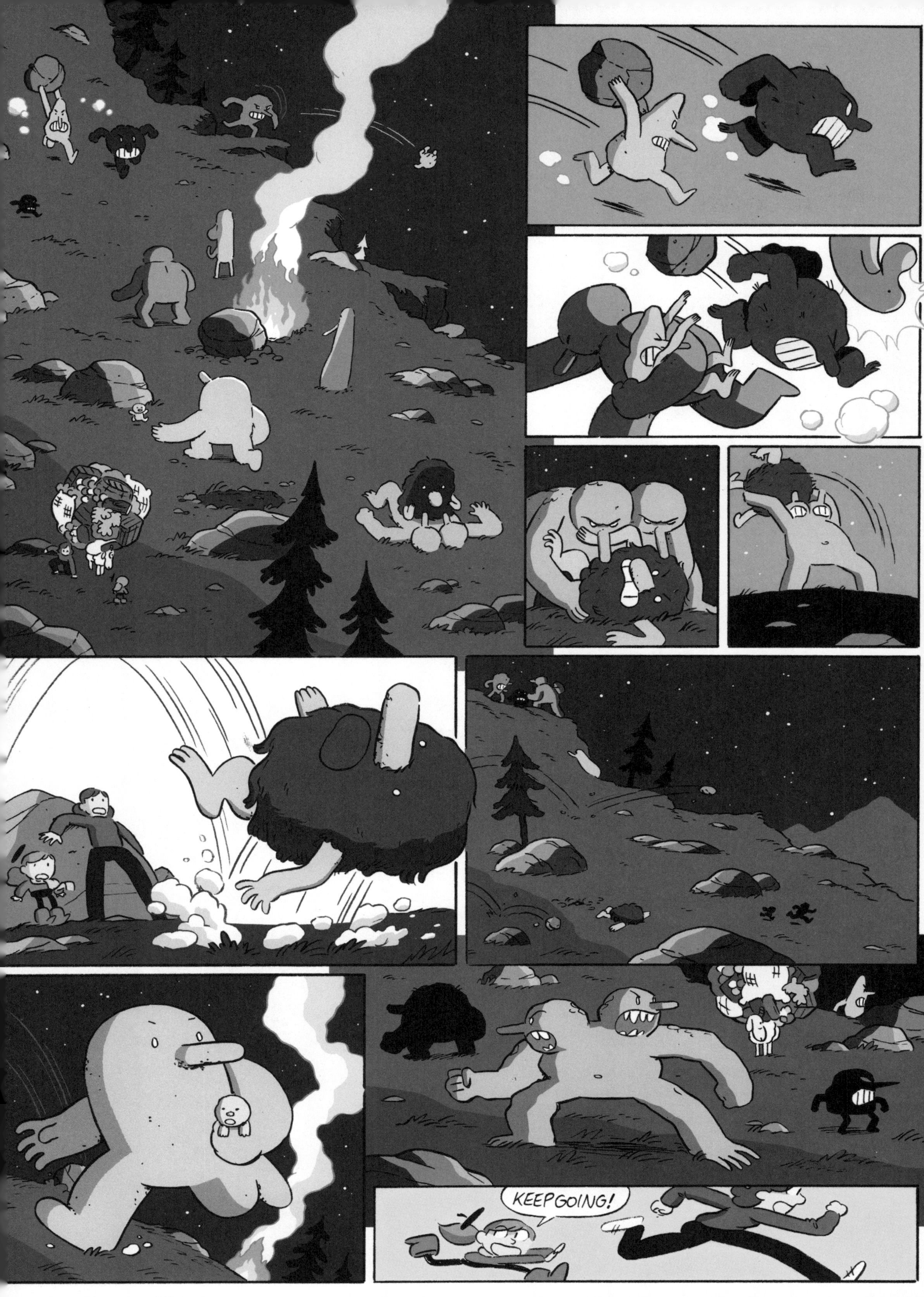
KEEP GOING!

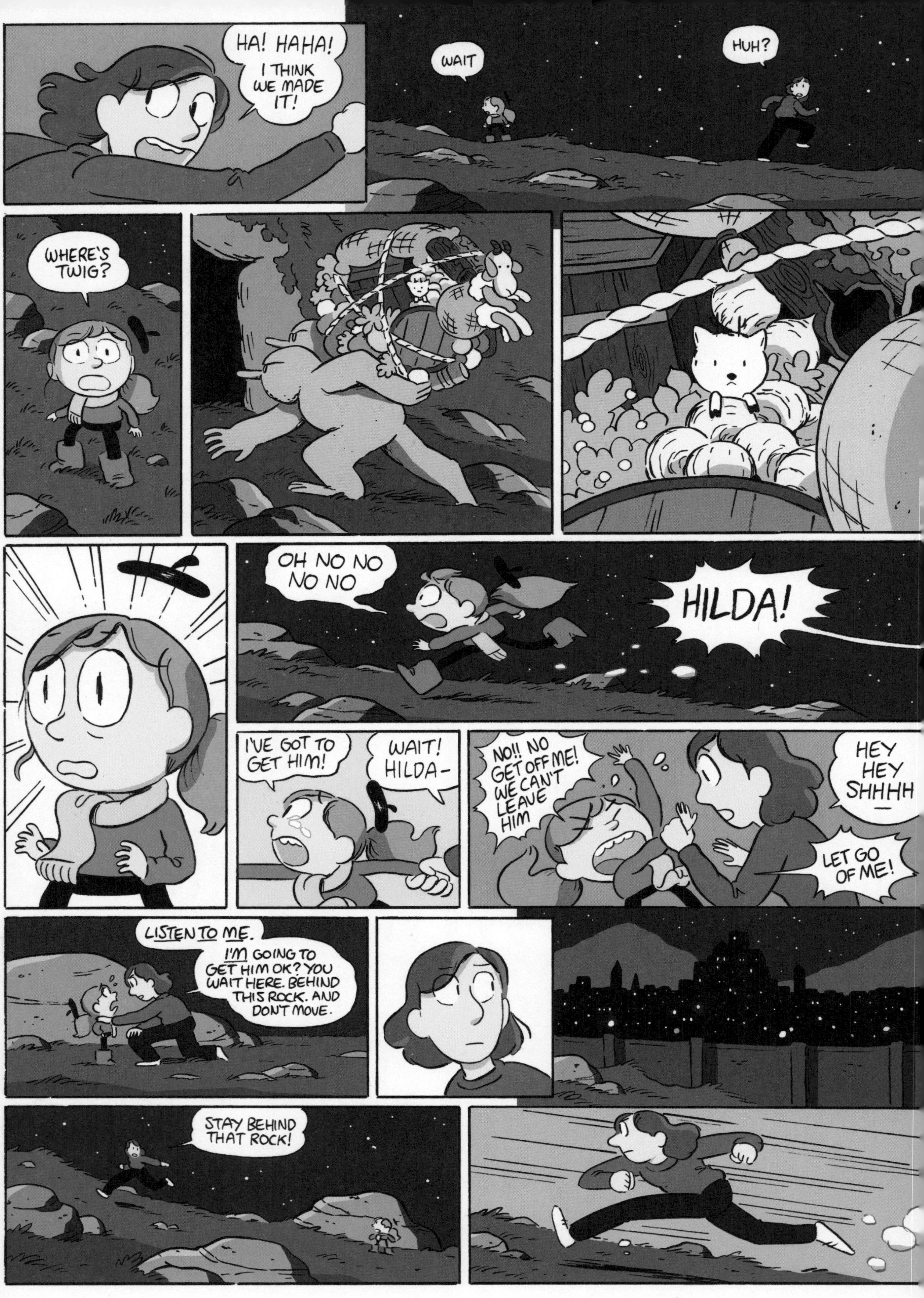

HA! HAHA!
I THINK WE MADE IT!
WAIT
HUH?
WHERE'S TWIG?
OH NO NO NO NO
HILDA!
I'VE GOT TO GET HIM!
WAIT! HILDA-
NO!! NO GET OFF ME! WE CAN'T LEAVE HIM
HEY HEY SHHHH –
LET GO OF ME!
LISTEN TO ME.
I'M GOING TO GET HIM OK? YOU WAIT HERE. BEHIND THIS ROCK. AND DON'T MOVE.
STAY BEHIND THAT ROCK!

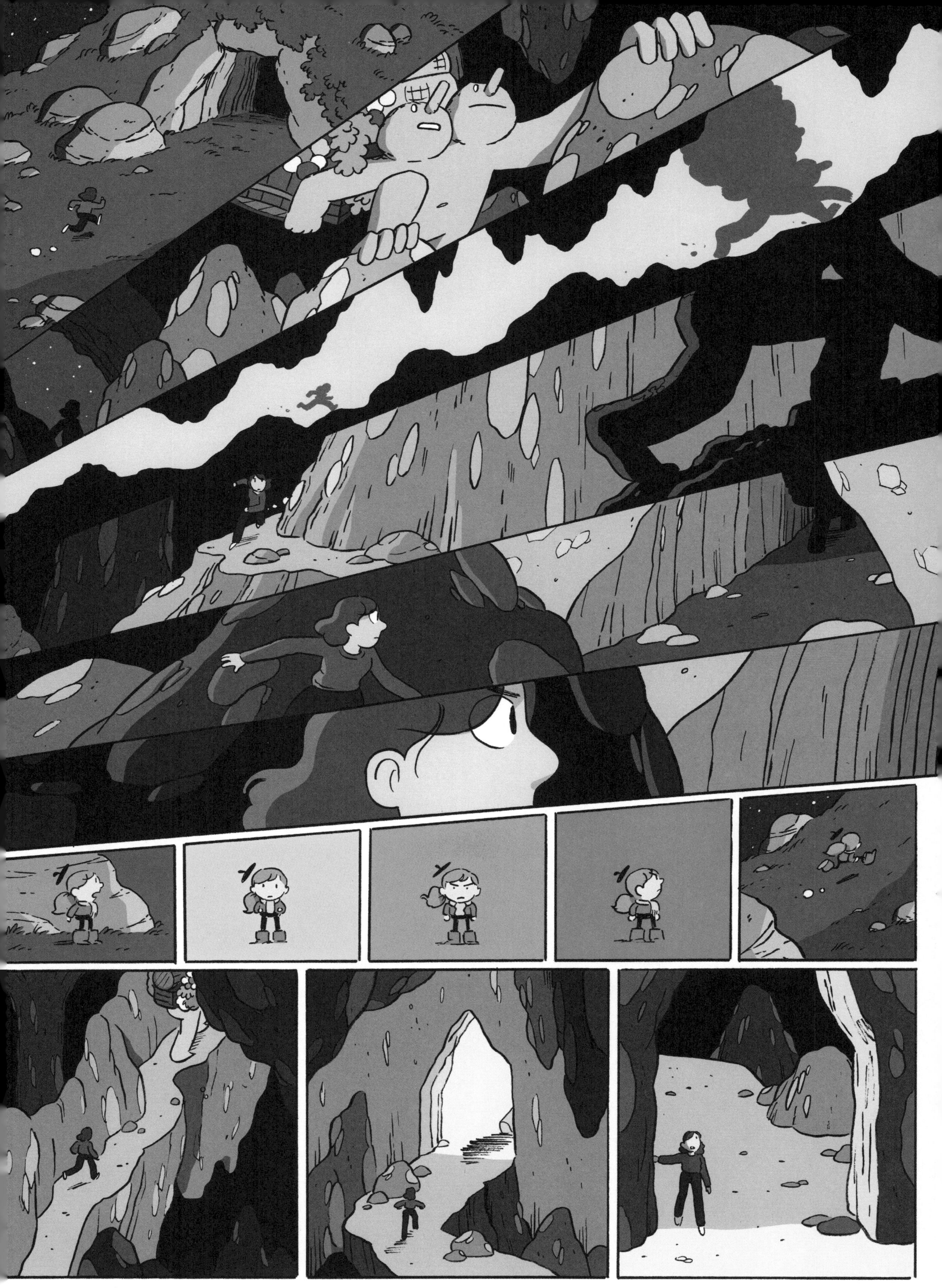

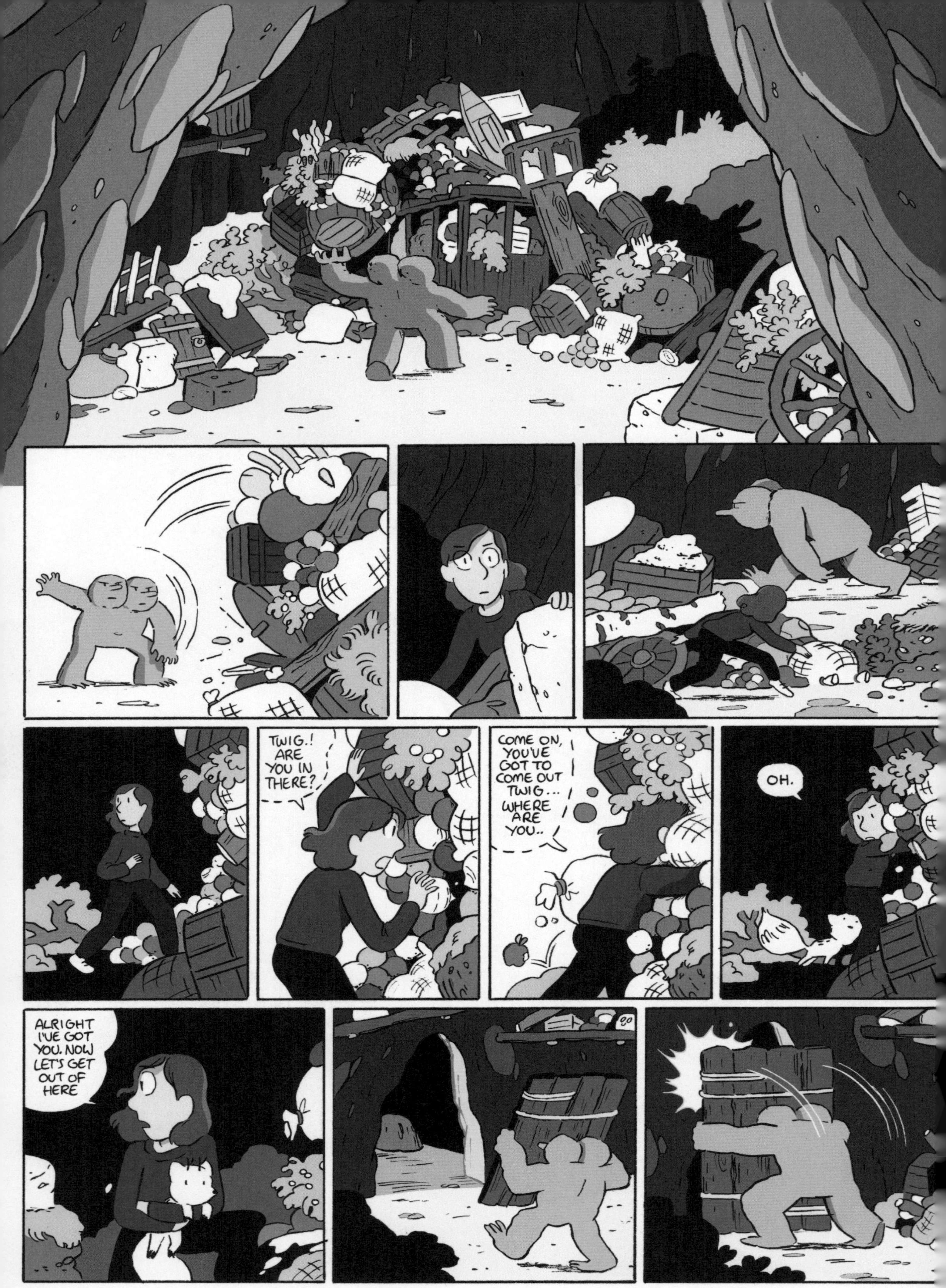
TWIG.! ARE YOU IN THERE?
COME ON, YOU'VE GOT TO COME OUT TWIG... WHERE ARE YOU..
OH.
ALRIGHT I'VE GOT YOU. NOW LET'S GET OUT OF HERE

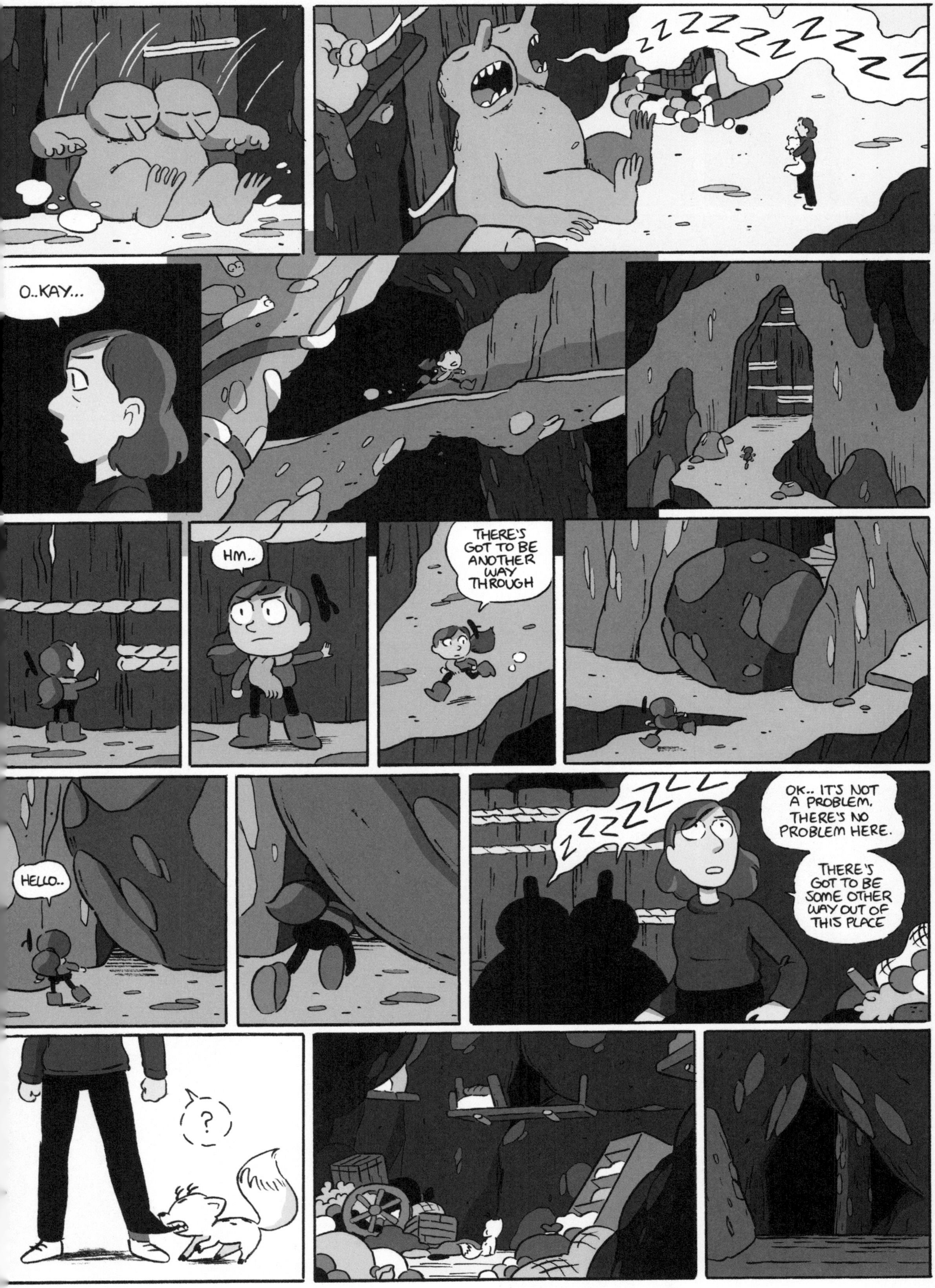

ZZZZZZZZZZZZ
O..KAY...
HM..
THERE'S GOT TO BE ANOTHER WAY THROUGH
HELLO..
ZZZZZZZZ
OK.. IT'S NOT A PROBLEM. THERE'S NO PROBLEM HERE.
THERE'S GOT TO BE SOME OTHER WAY OUT OF THIS PLACE
?

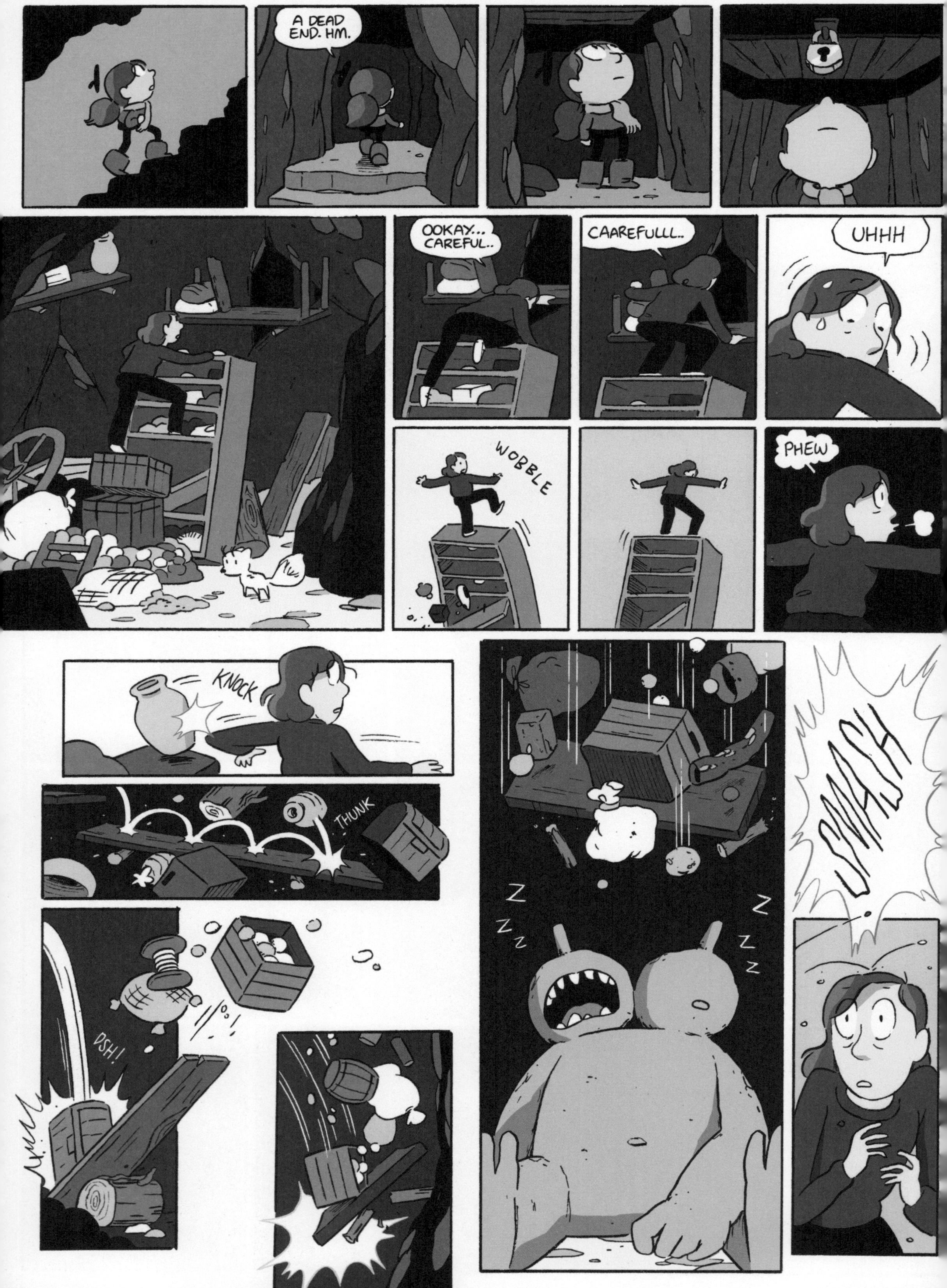

A DEAD END. HM.
OOKAY... CAREFUL..
CAAREFULLL..
UHHH
WOBBLE
PHEW
KNOCK
THUNK
DSH!
SMASH
Z
Z Z
Z
Z Z

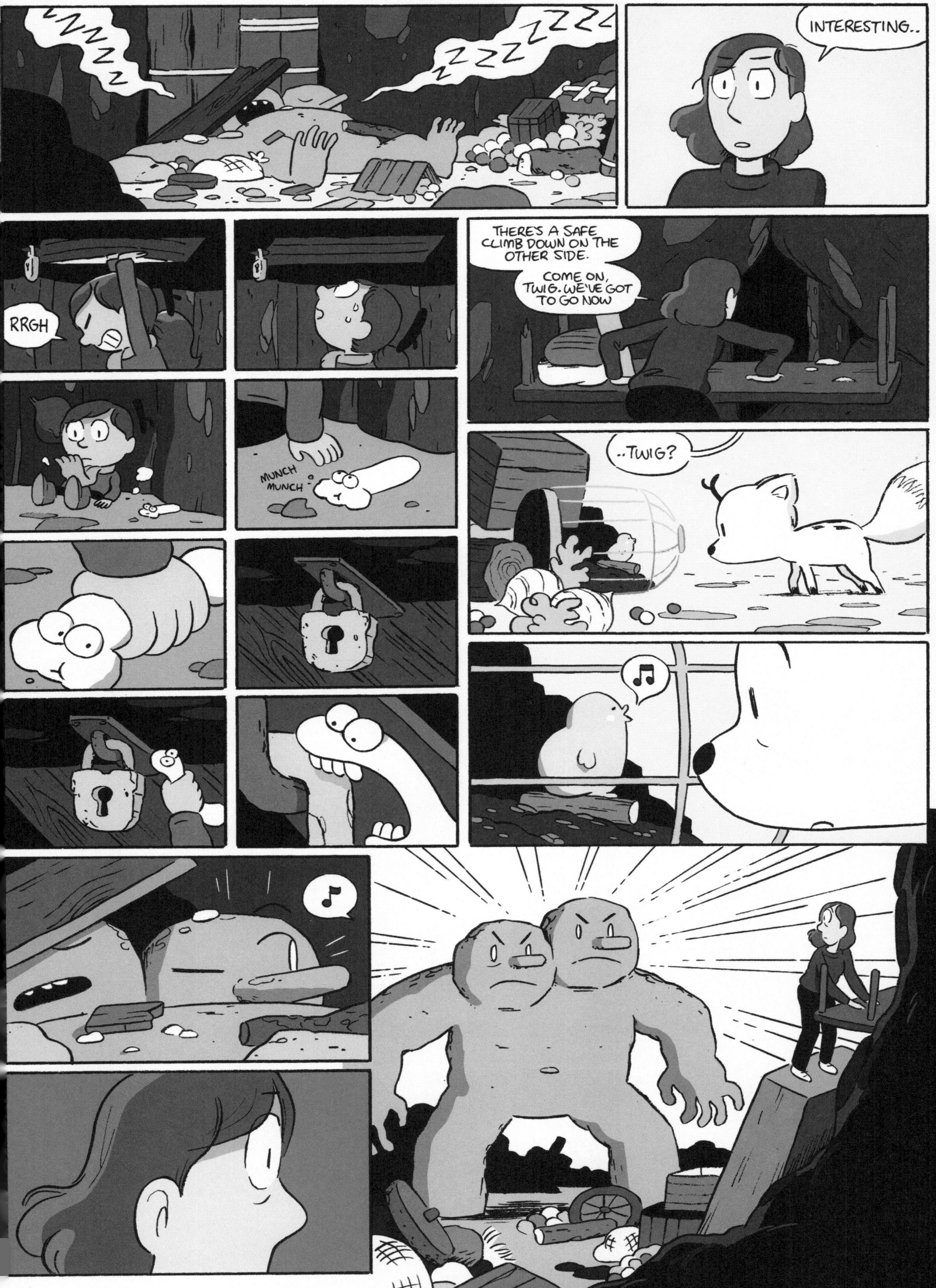

INTERESTING..
RRGH
THERE'S A SAFE CLIMB DOWN ON THE OTHER SIDE.
COME ON, TWIG. WE'VE GOT TO GO NOW
MUNCH MUNCH
..TWIG?

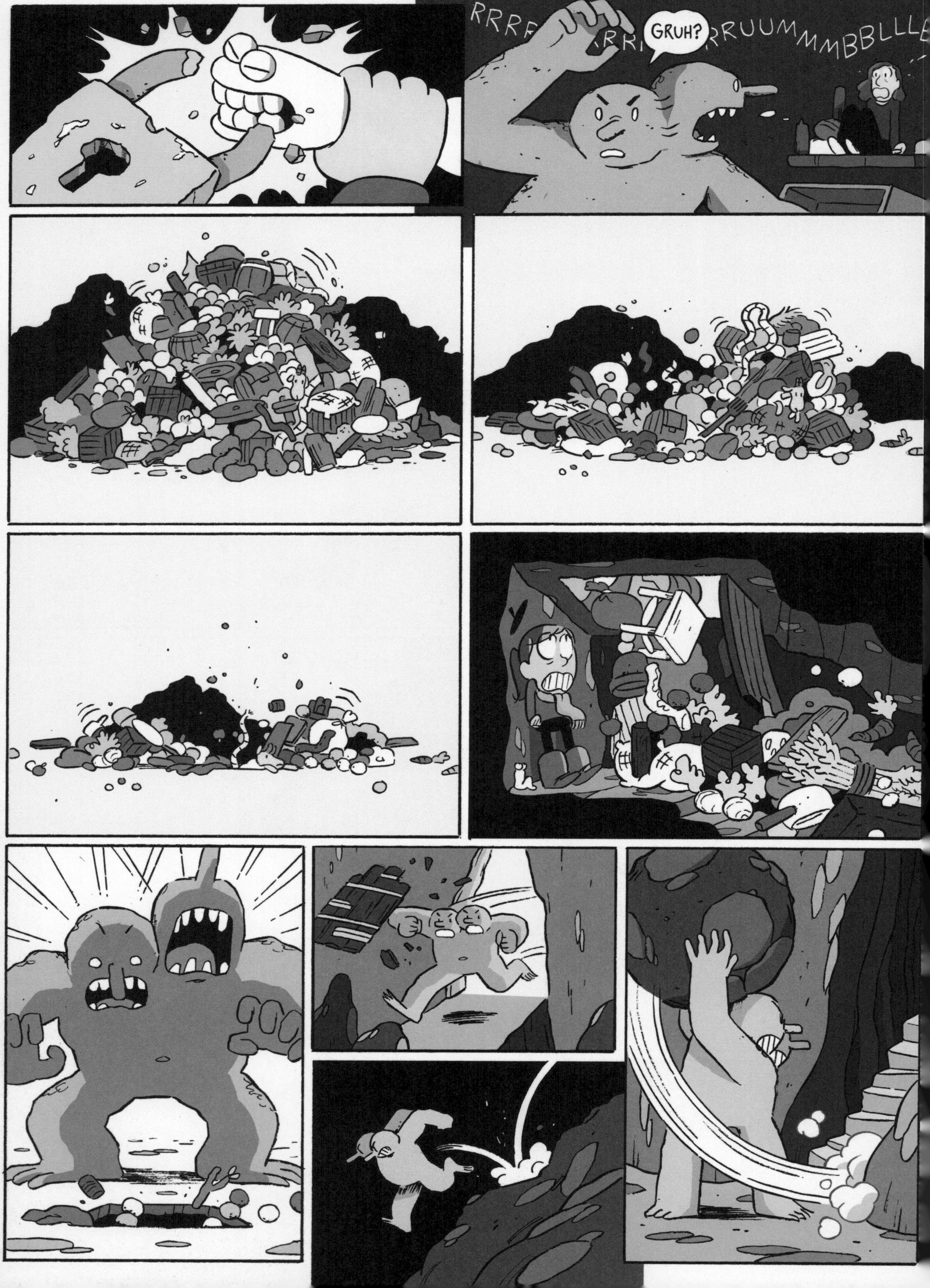

RRRR
GRUH?
RRRRUUMMMBBLLLE

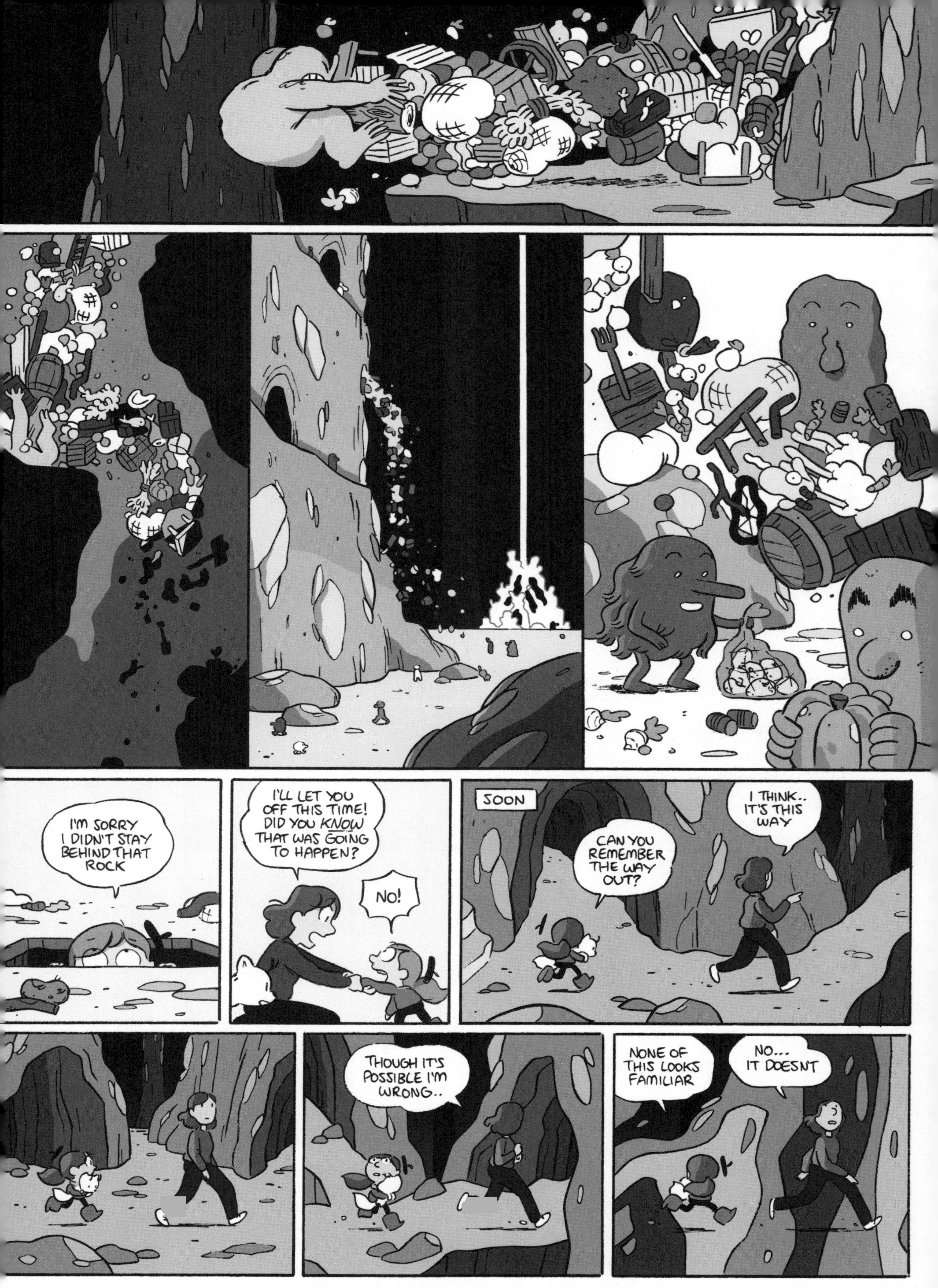
I'M SORRY I DIDN'T STAY BEHIND THAT ROCK
I'LL LET YOU OFF THIS TIME! DID YOU KNOW THAT WAS GOING TO HAPPEN?
NO!
SOON
CAN YOU REMEMBER THE WAY OUT?
I THINK.. IT'S THIS WAY
THOUGH IT'S POSSIBLE I'M WRONG..
NONE OF THIS LOOKS FAMILIAR
NO... IT DOESNT

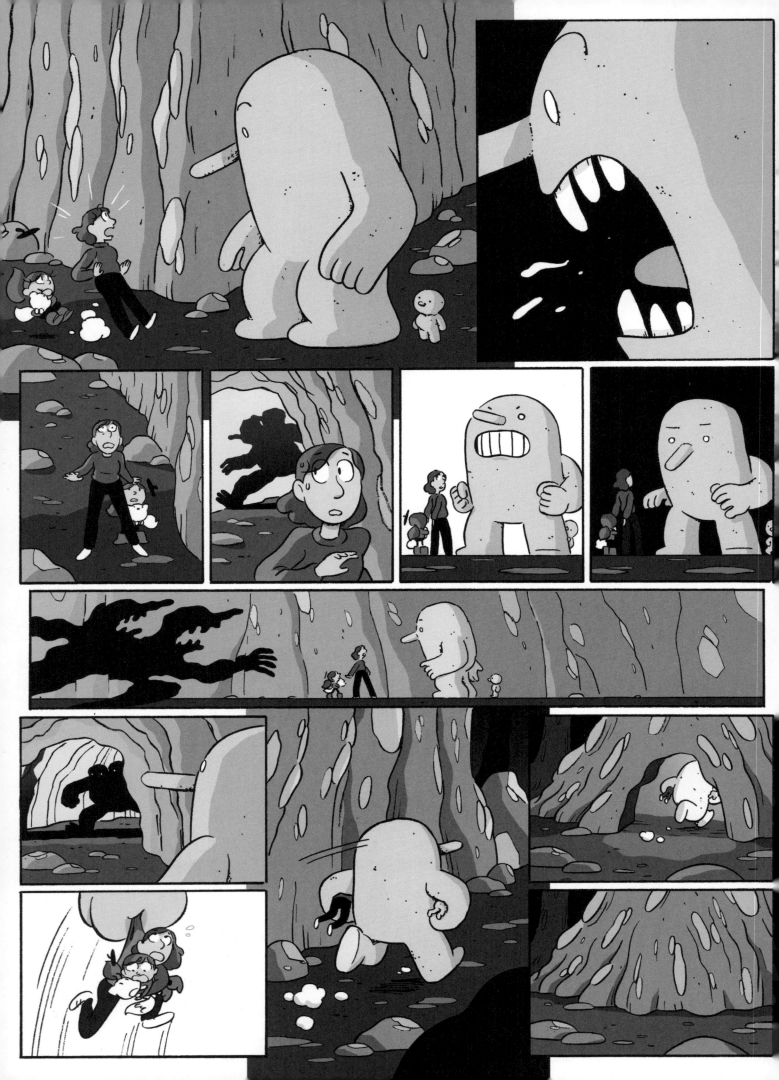

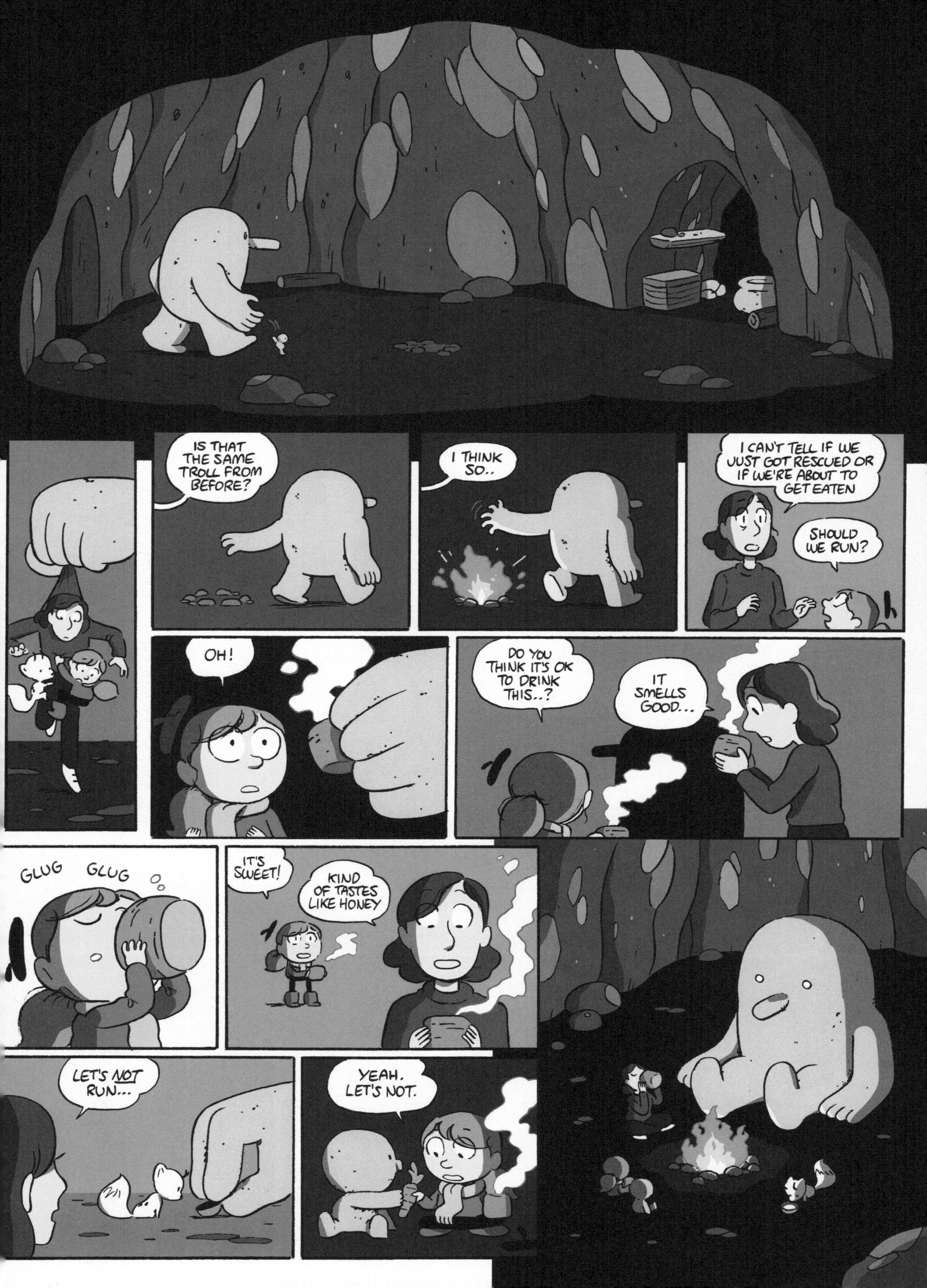
IS THAT THE SAME TROLL FROM BEFORE?
I THINK SO..
I CAN'T TELL IF WE JUST GOT RESCUED OR IF WE'RE ABOUT TO GET EATEN
SHOULD WE RUN?
OH!
DO YOU THINK IT'S OK TO DRINK THIS..?
IT SMELLS GOOD...
GLUG GLUG
IT'S SWEET!
KIND OF TASTES LIKE HONEY
LET'S NOT RUN...
YEAH. LET'S NOT.

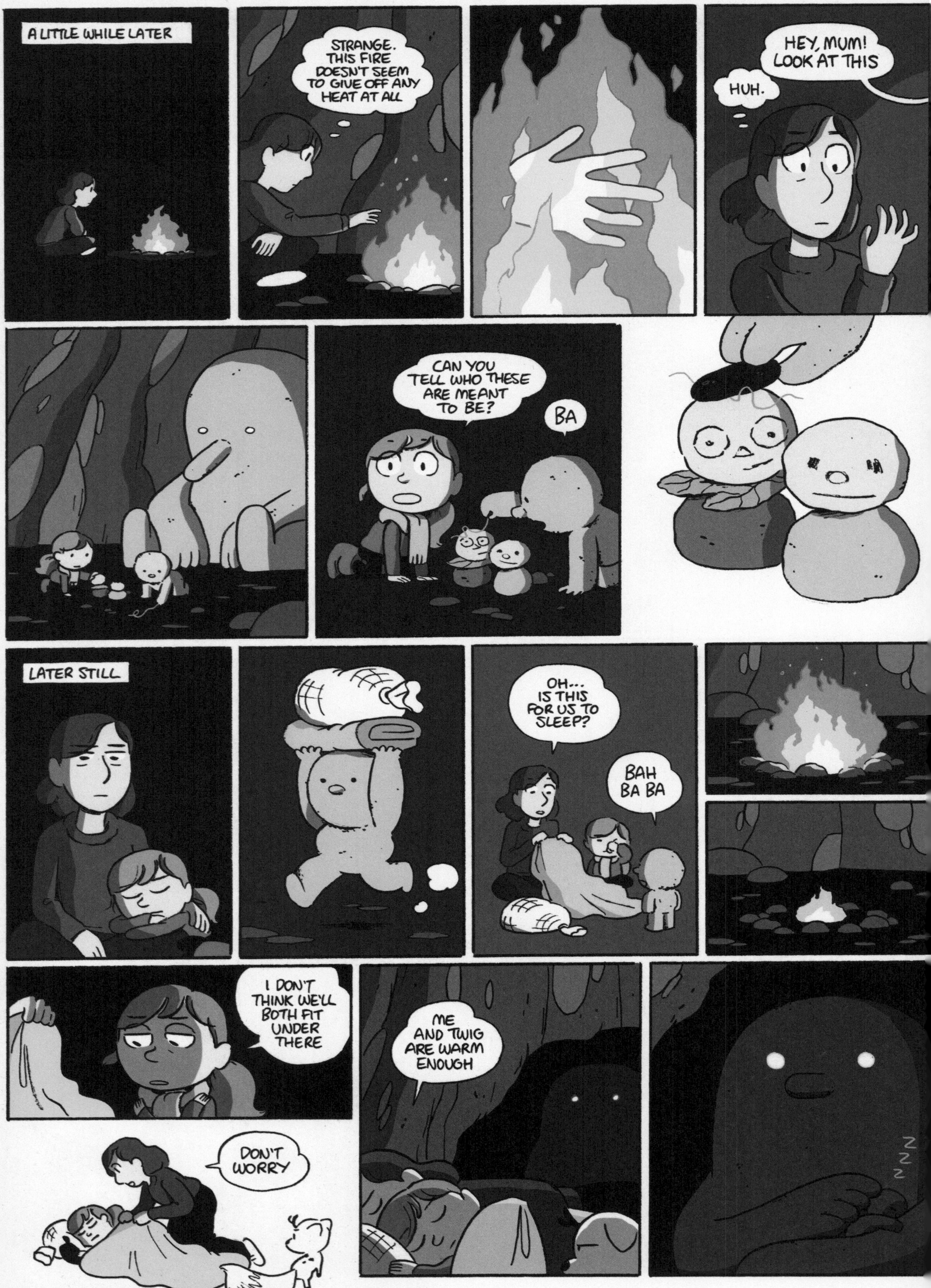

A LITTLE WHILE LATER
STRANGE. THIS FIRE DOESN'T SEEM TO GIVE OFF ANY HEAT AT ALL
HEY, MUM! LOOK AT THIS
HUH.
CAN YOU TELL WHO THESE ARE MEANT TO BE?
BA
LATER STILL
OH... IS THIS FOR US TO SLEEP?
BAH BA BA
I DON'T THINK WE'LL BOTH FIT UNDER THERE
DON'T WORRY
ME AND TWIG ARE WARM ENOUGH
ZZZ

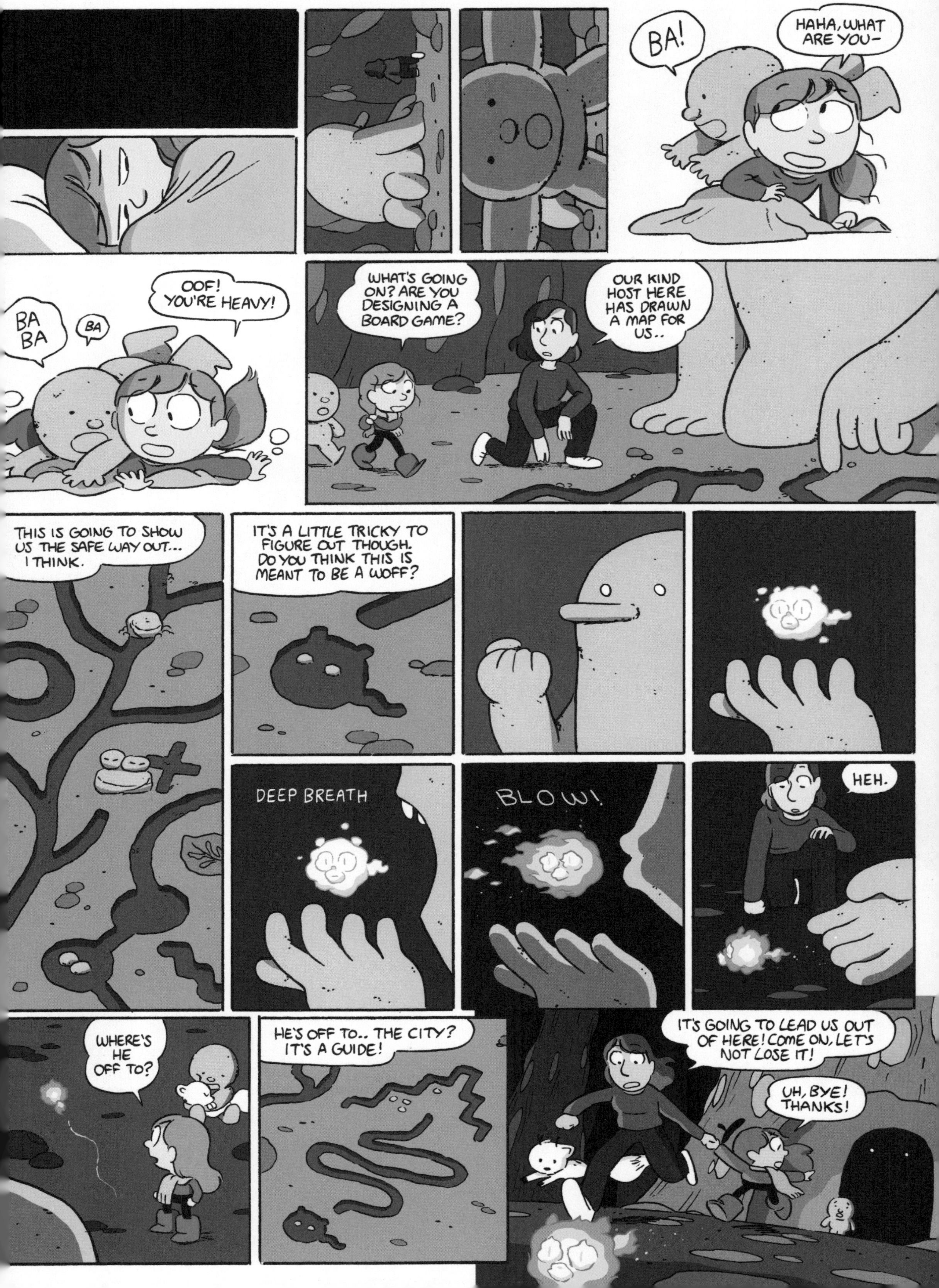
BA!
HAHA, WHAT ARE YOU-
OOF! YOU'RE HEAVY!
BA BA
BA
WHAT'S GOING ON? ARE YOU DESIGNING A BOARD GAME?
OUR KIND HOST HERE HAS DRAWN A MAP FOR US..
THIS IS GOING TO SHOW US THE SAFE WAY OUT... I THINK.
IT'S A LITTLE TRICKY TO FIGURE OUT THOUGH. DO YOU THINK THIS IS MEANT TO BE A WOFF?
DEEP BREATH
BLOW!
HEH.
WHERE'S HE OFF TO?
HE'S OFF TO.. THE CITY? IT'S A GUIDE!
IT'S GOING TO LEAD US OUT OF HERE! COME ON, LET'S NOT LOSE IT!
UH, BYE! THANKS!

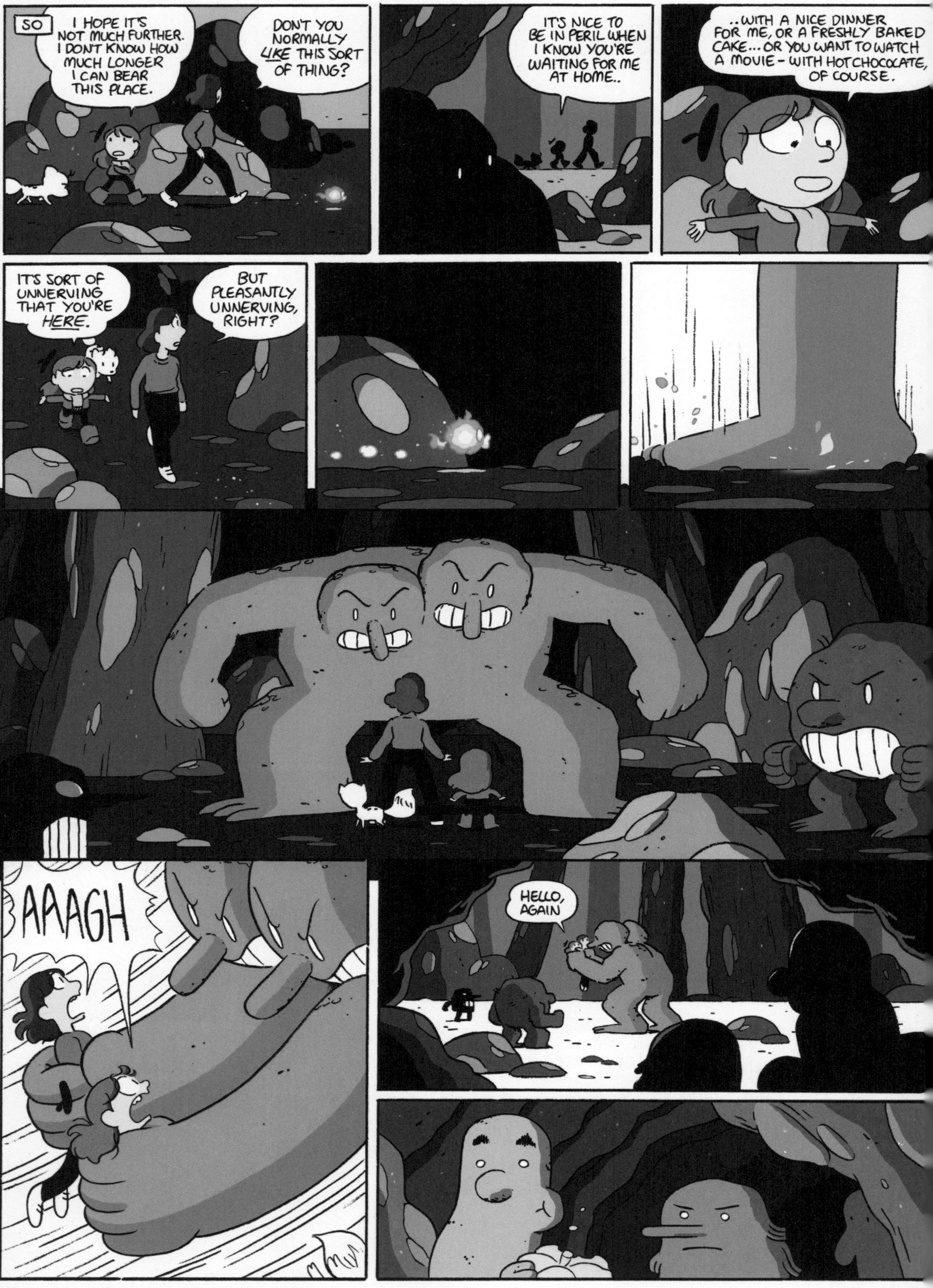

SO
I HOPE IT'S NOT MUCH FURTHER. I DON'T KNOW HOW MUCH LONGER I CAN BEAR THIS PLACE.
DON'T YOU NORMALLY LIKE THIS SORT OF THING?
IT'S NICE TO BE IN PERIL WHEN I KNOW YOU'RE WAITING FOR ME AT HOME..
..WITH A NICE DINNER FOR ME, OR A FRESHLY BAKED CAKE... OR YOU WANT TO WATCH A MOVIE - WITH HOT CHOCOCATE, OF COURSE.
IT'S SORT OF UNNERVING THAT YOU'RE HERE.
BUT PLEASANTLY UNNERVING, RIGHT?
AAAGH
HELLO, AGAIN

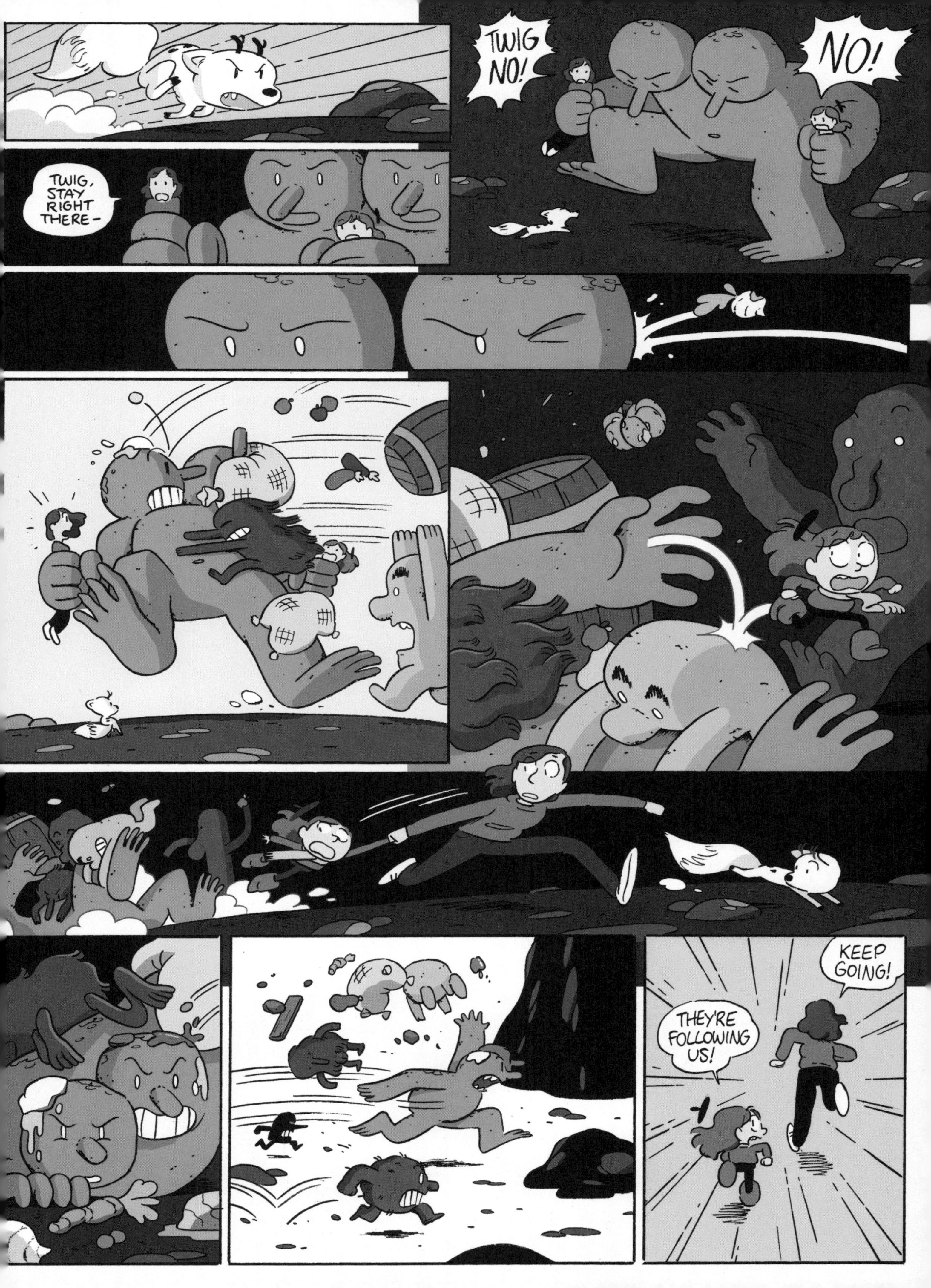
TWIG, STAY RIGHT THERE-
TWIG NO!
NO!
KEEP GOING!
THEY'RE FOLLOWING US!

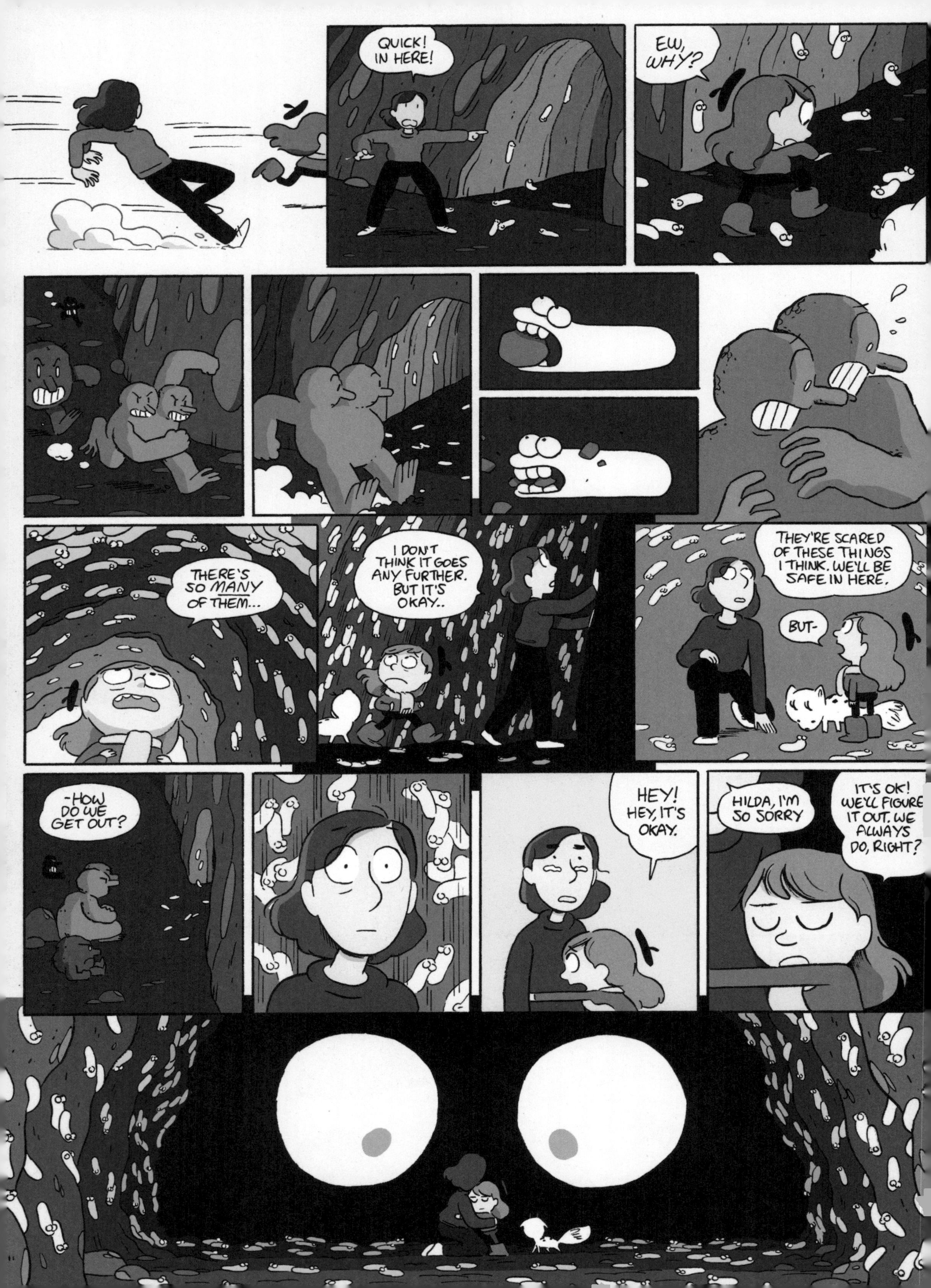
QUICK! IN HERE!
EW, WHY?
THERE'S SO MANY OF THEM...
I DON'T THINK IT GOES ANY FURTHER. BUT IT'S OKAY..
THEY'RE SCARED OF THESE THINGS I THINK. WE'LL BE SAFE IN HERE.
BUT-
-HOW DO WE GET OUT?
HEY! HEY, IT'S OKAY.
HILDA, I'M SO SORRY
IT'S OK! WE'LL FIGURE IT OUT. WE ALWAYS DO, RIGHT?

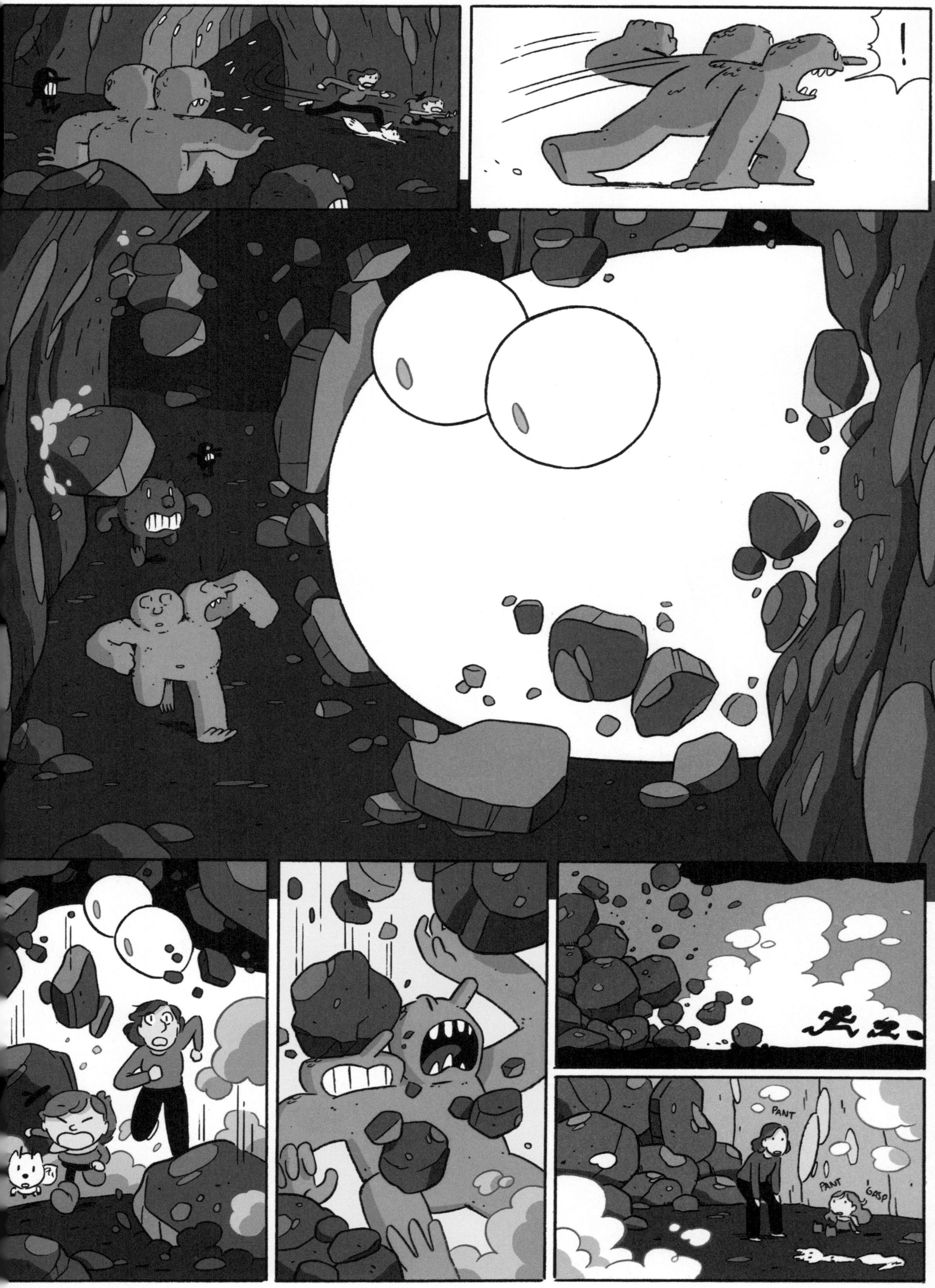
!
PANT
PANT
GASP

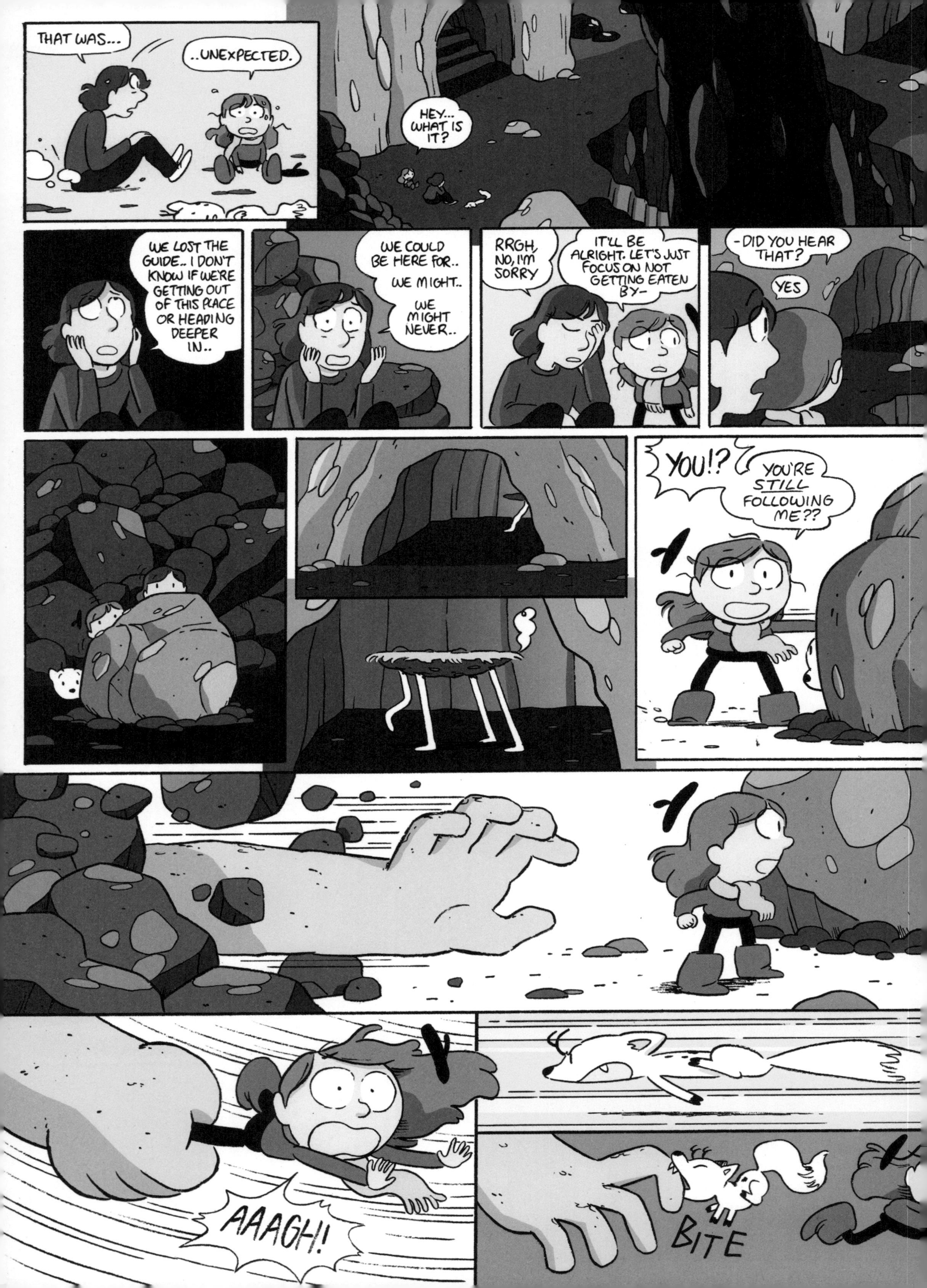
THAT WAS...
..UNEXPECTED.
HEY... WHAT IS IT?
WE LOST THE GUIDE.. I DON'T KNOW IF WE'RE GETTING OUT OF THIS PLACE OR HEADING DEEPER IN..
WE COULD BE HERE FOR..
WE MIGHT..
WE MIGHT NEVER..
RRGH, NO, I'M SORRY
IT'LL BE ALRIGHT. LET'S JUST FOCUS ON NOT GETTING EATEN BY-
-DID YOU HEAR THAT?
YES
YOU!?
YOU'RE STILL FOLLOWING ME??
AAAGH!
BITE

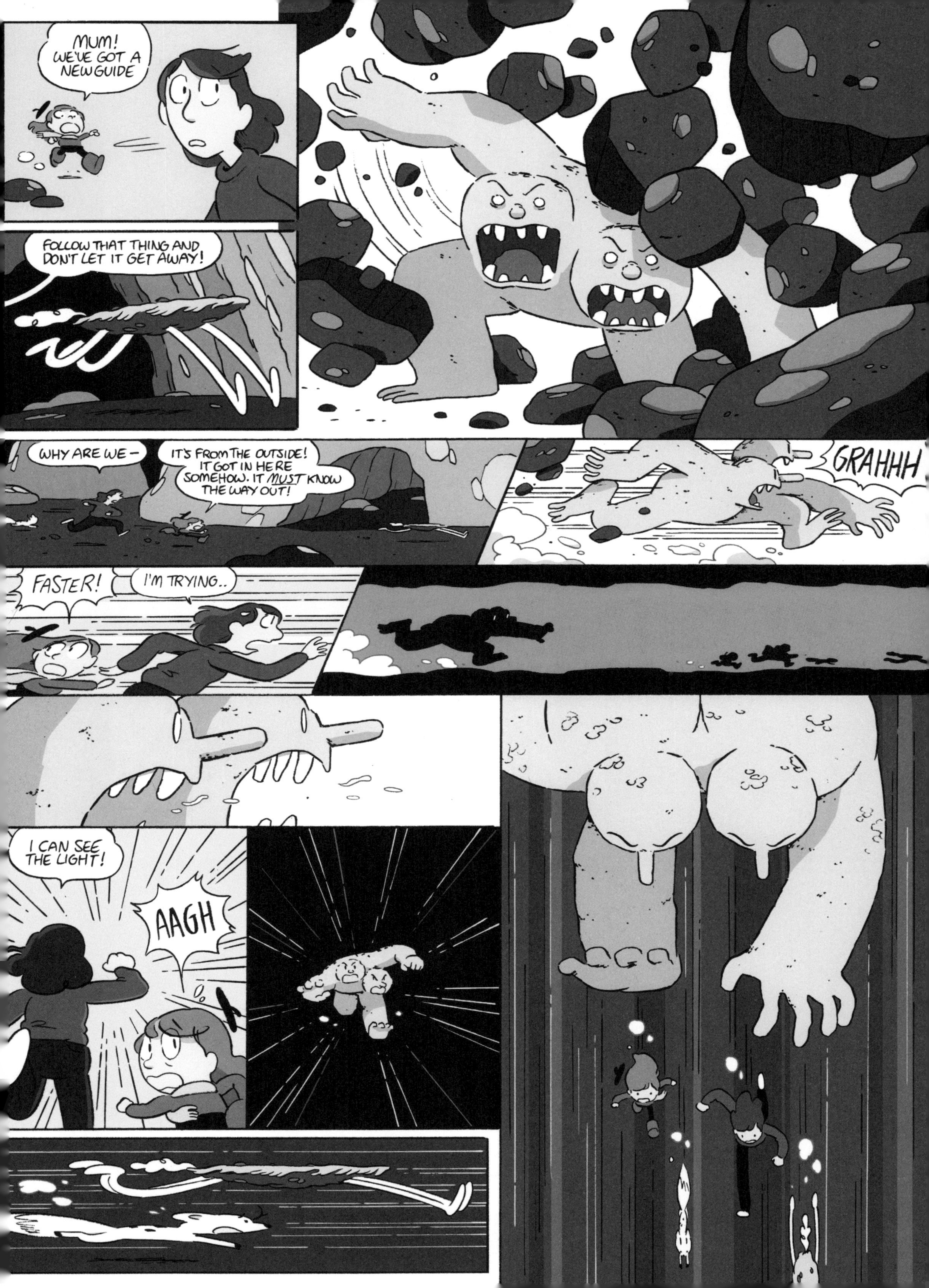
MUM! WE'VE GOT A NEW GUIDE
FOLLOW THAT THING AND DON'T LET IT GET AWAY!
WHY ARE WE -
IT'S FROM THE OUTSIDE! IT GOT IN HERE SOMEHOW. IT MUST KNOW THE WAY OUT!
GRAHHH
FASTER!
I'M TRYING..
I CAN SEE THE LIGHT!
AAGH

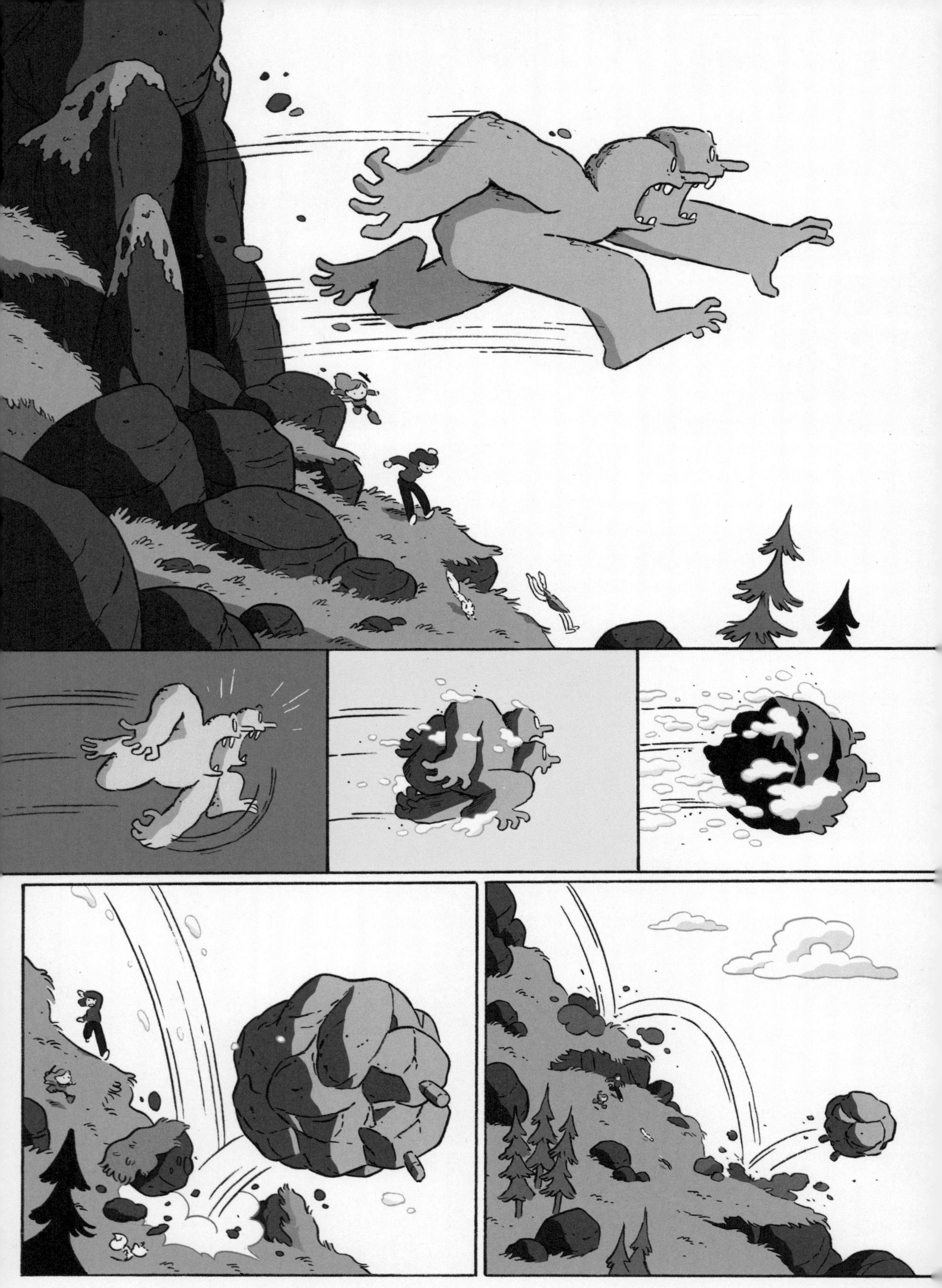

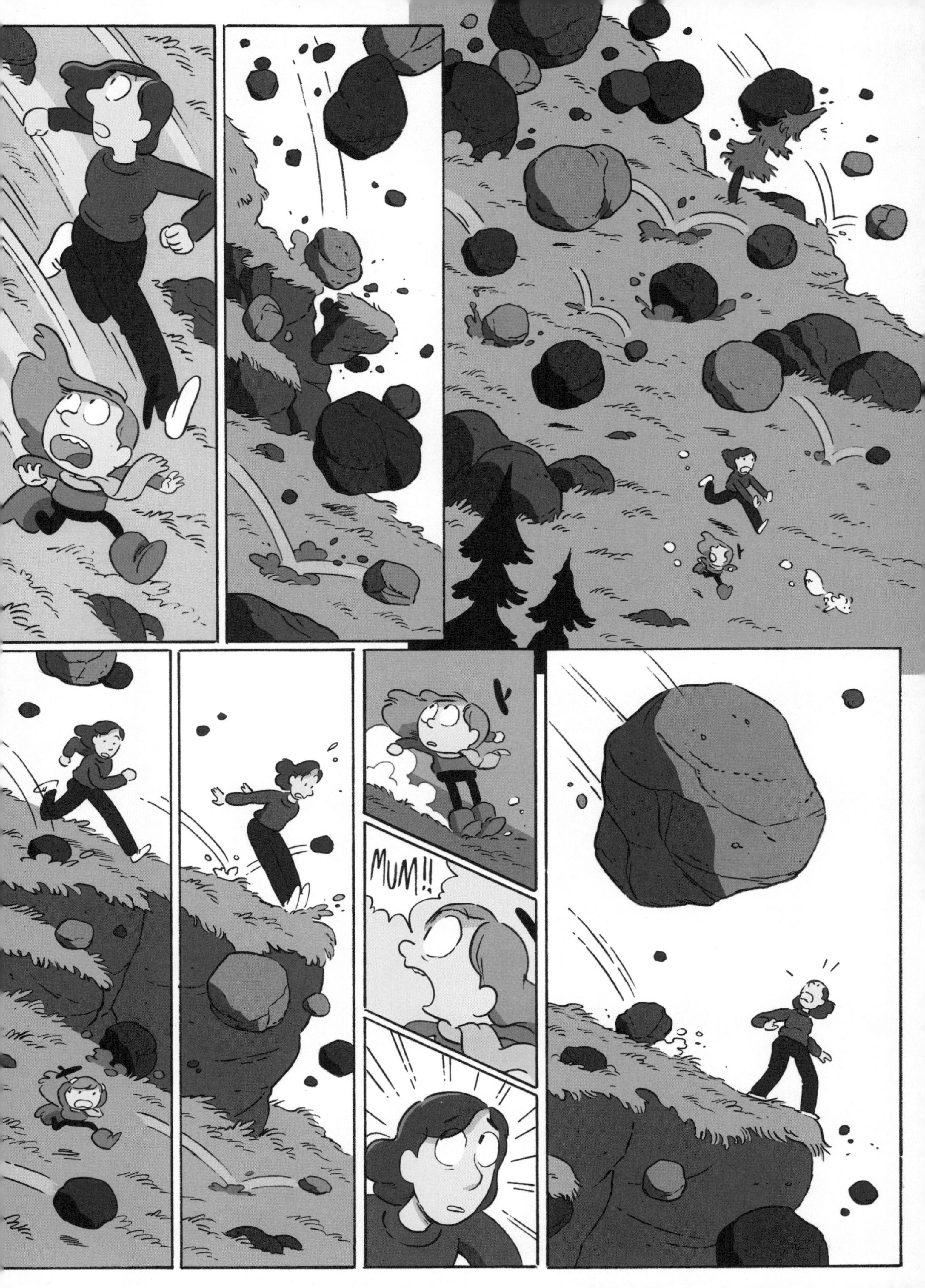
MUM!!

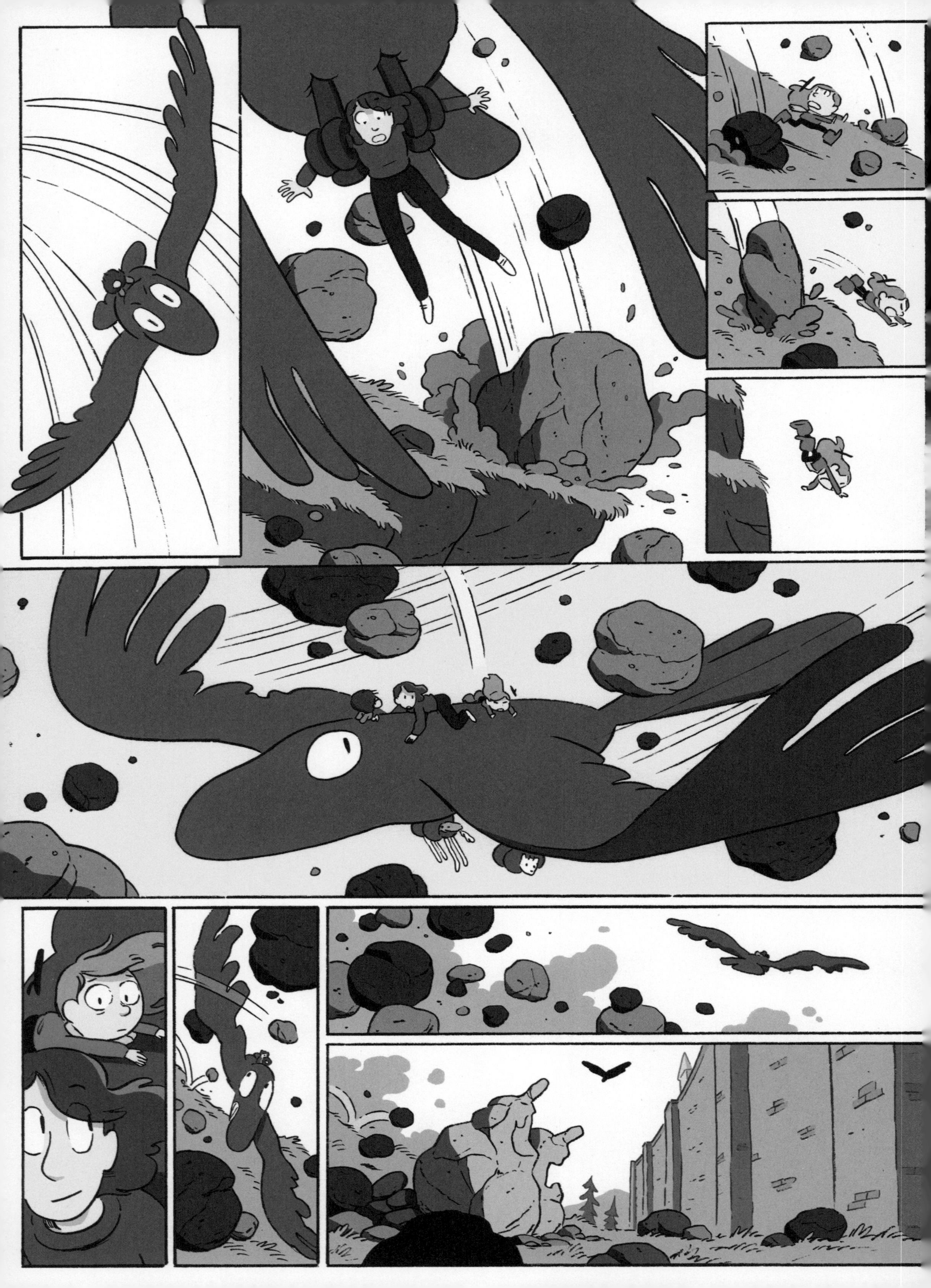

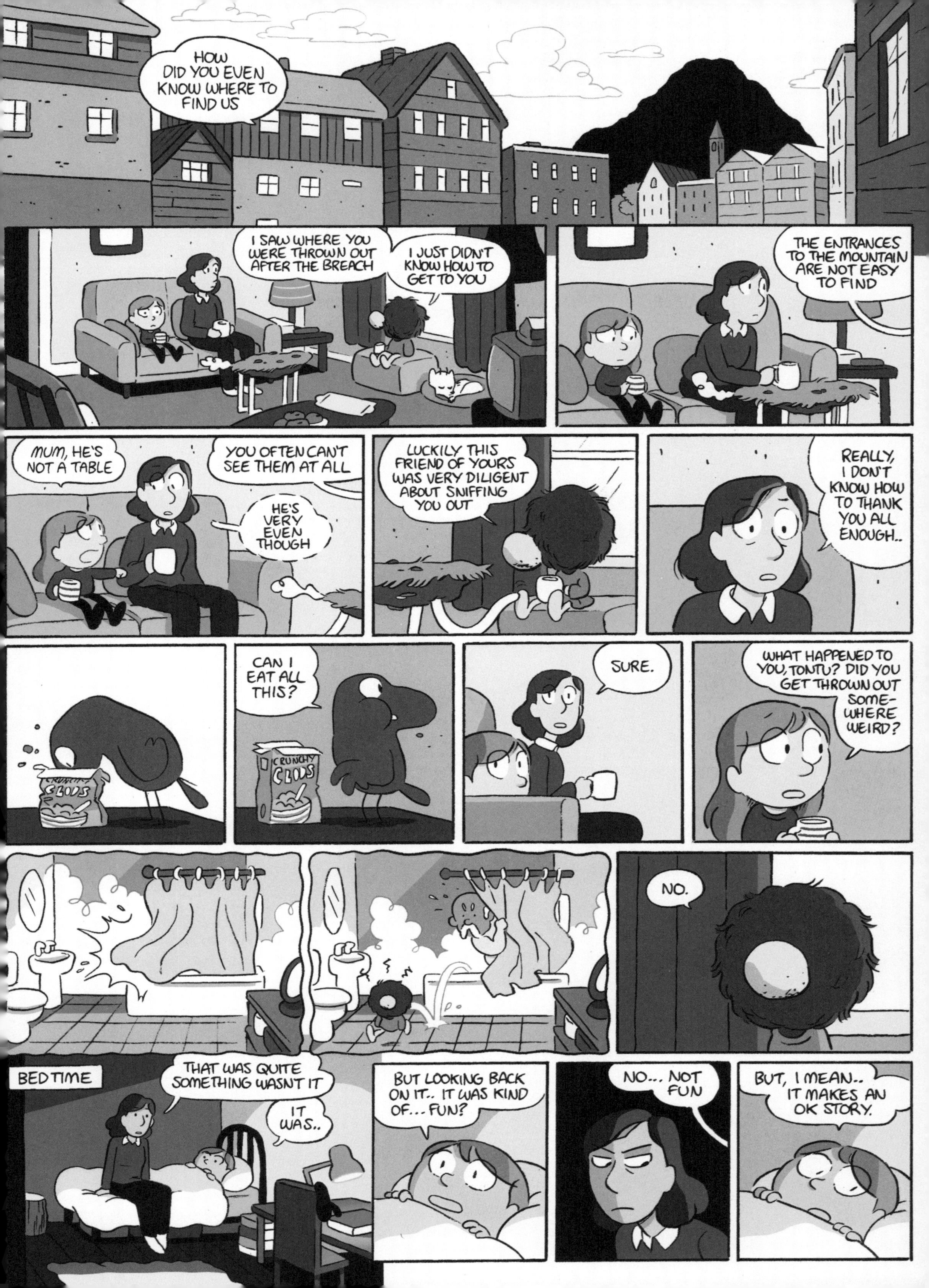

HOW DID YOU EVEN KNOW WHERE TO FIND US
I SAW WHERE YOU WERE THROWN OUT AFTER THE BREACH
I JUST DIDN'T KNOW HOW TO GET TO YOU
THE ENTRANCES TO THE MOUNTAIN ARE NOT EASY TO FIND
MUM, HE'S NOT A TABLE
YOU OFTEN CAN'T SEE THEM AT ALL
HE'S VERY EVEN THOUGH
LUCKILY THIS FRIEND OF YOURS WAS VERY DILIGENT ABOUT SNIFFING YOU OUT
REALLY, I DON'T KNOW HOW TO THANK YOU ALL ENOUGH..
CAN I EAT ALL THIS?
CRUNCHY CLODS
SURE.
WHAT HAPPENED TO YOU, TONTU? DID YOU GET THROWN OUT SOME-WHERE WEIRD?
NO.
BEDTIME
THAT WAS QUITE SOMETHING WASNT IT
IT WAS..
BUT LOOKING BACK ON IT.. IT WAS KIND OF... FUN?
NO... NOT FUN
BUT, I MEAN.. IT MAKES AN OK STORY.

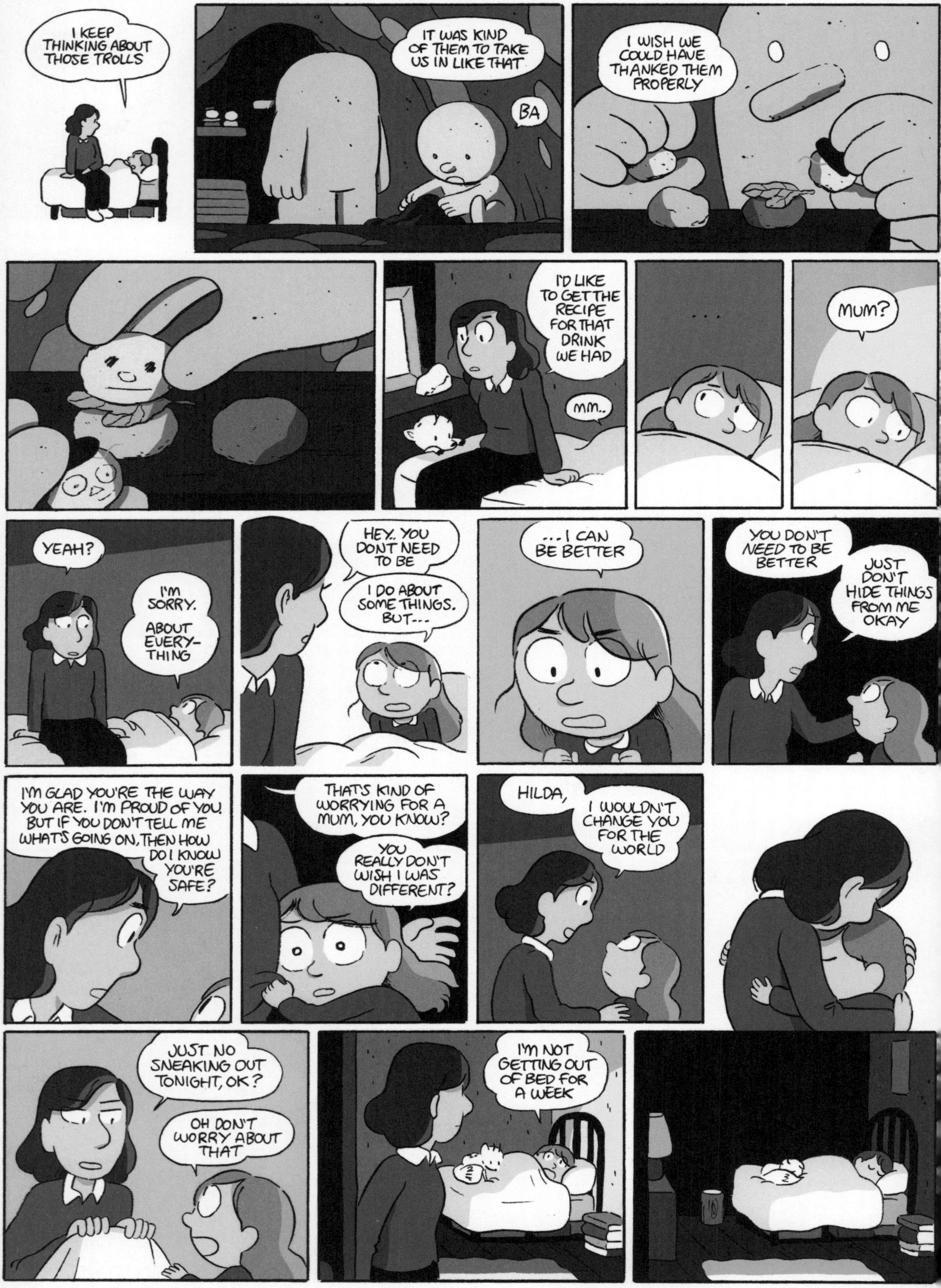
I KEEP THINKING ABOUT THOSE TROLLS
IT WAS KIND OF THEM TO TAKE US IN LIKE THAT
BA
I WISH WE COULD HAVE THANKED THEM PROPERLY
I'D LIKE TO GET THE RECIPE FOR THAT DRINK WE HAD
MM..
...
MUM?
YEAH?
I'M SORRY. ABOUT EVERY-THING
HEY.. YOU DONT NEED TO BE
I DO ABOUT SOME THINGS. BUT...
...I CAN BE BETTER
YOU DON'T NEED TO BE BETTER
JUST DON'T HIDE THINGS FROM ME OKAY
I'M GLAD YOU'RE THE WAY YOU ARE. I'M PROUD OF YOU. BUT IF YOU DON'T TELL ME WHAT'S GOING ON, THEN HOW DO I KNOW YOU'RE SAFE?
THAT'S KIND OF WORRYING FOR A MUM, YOU KNOW?
YOU REALLY DON'T WISH I WAS DIFFERENT?
HILDA,
I WOULDN'T CHANGE YOU FOR THE WORLD
JUST NO SNEAKING OUT TONIGHT, OK?
OH DON'T WORRY ABOUT THAT
I'M NOT GETTING OUT OF BED FOR A WEEK

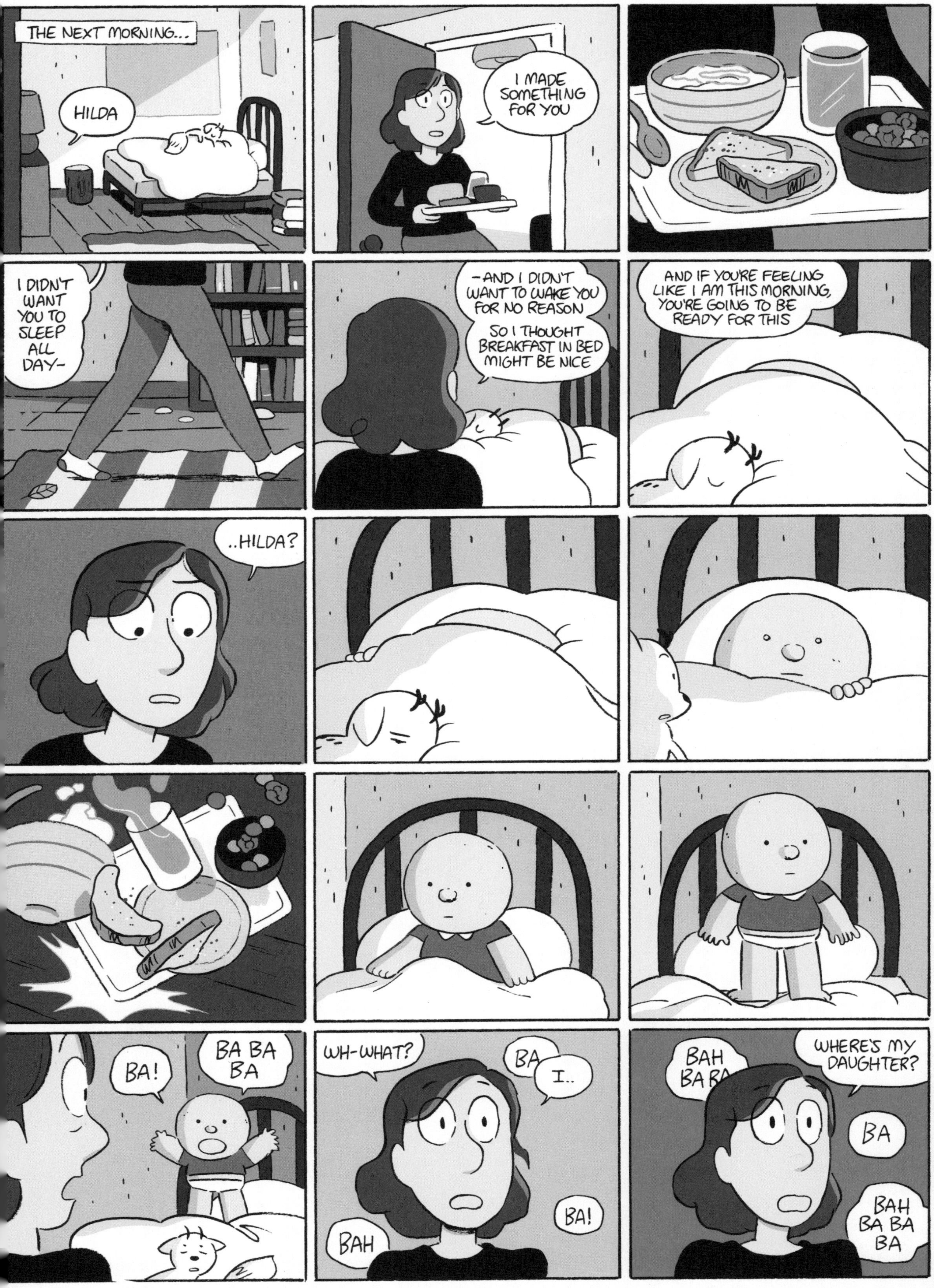
THE NEXT MORNING...
HILDA
I MADE SOMETHING FOR YOU
I DIDN'T WANT YOU TO SLEEP ALL DAY-
-AND I DIDN'T WANT TO WAKE YOU FOR NO REASON
SO I THOUGHT BREAKFAST IN BED MIGHT BE NICE
AND IF YOU'RE FEELING LIKE I AM THIS MORNING, YOU'RE GOING TO BE READY FOR THIS
..HILDA?
BA!
BA BA BA
WH-WHAT?
BA
I..
BA!
BAH
BAH BA BA
WHERE'S MY DAUGHTER?
BA
BAH BA BA BA

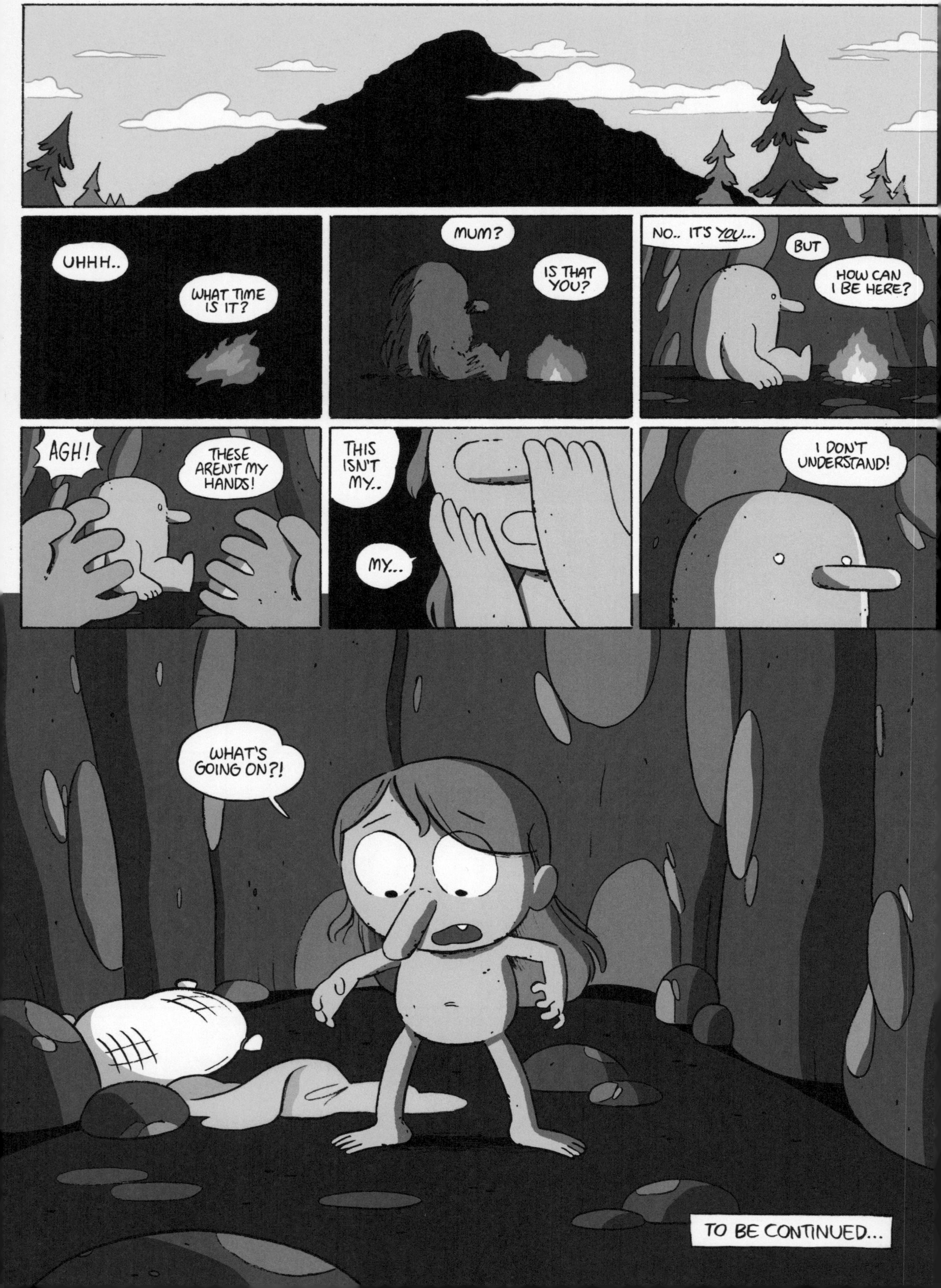
UHHH..
WHAT TIME IS IT?
MUM?
IS THAT YOU?
NO.. IT'S YOU...
BUT
HOW CAN I BE HERE?
AGH!
THESE AREN'T MY HANDS!
THIS ISN'T MY..
MY...
I DON'T UNDERSTAND!
WHAT'S GOING ON?!
TO BE CONTINUED...

JOIN THE ADVENTURES OF OUR FAVOURITE BLUE-HAIRED HEROINE IN THE WORLD OF HILDAFOLK!

HILDA AND THE TROLL
HARDBACK ISBN 978-1-909263-14-7
PAPERBACK ISBN 978-1-909263-78-9

HILDA AND THE MIDNIGHT GIANT
HARDBACK ISBN 978-1-909263-17-8
PAPERBACK ISBN 978-1-909263-79-6

HILDA AND THE BIRD PARADE
HARDBACK ISBN 978-1-909263-06-2
PAPERBACK ISBN 978-1-911171-02-7

HILDA AND THE BLACK HOUND
HARDBACK ISBN 978-1-909263-18-5
PAPERBACK 978-1-911171-07-2

OUR HEROINE IS TRAPPED IN THE BODY OF A TROLL! HER MUM IS WORRIED SICK, AND PERPLEXED BY THE STRANGE CREATURE THAT HAS TAKEN HILDA'S PLACE.

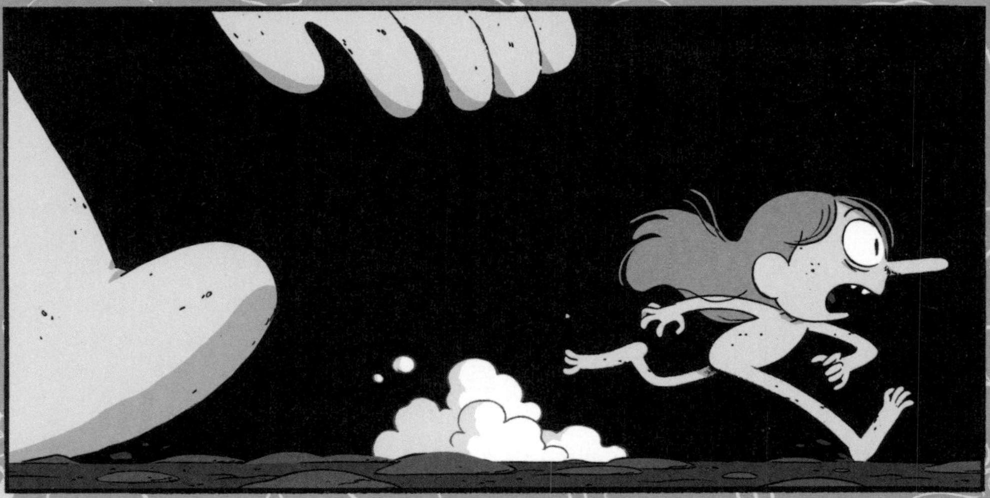

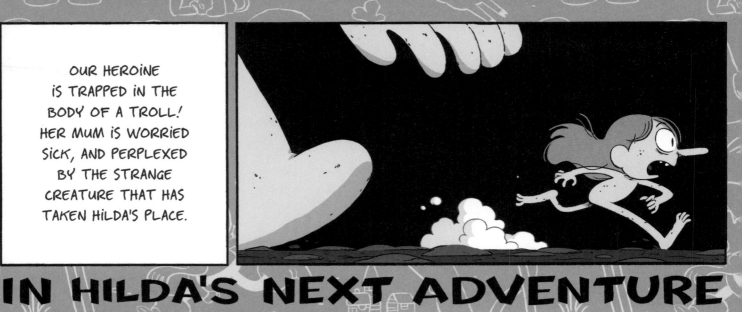

IN HILDA'S NEXT ADVENTURE

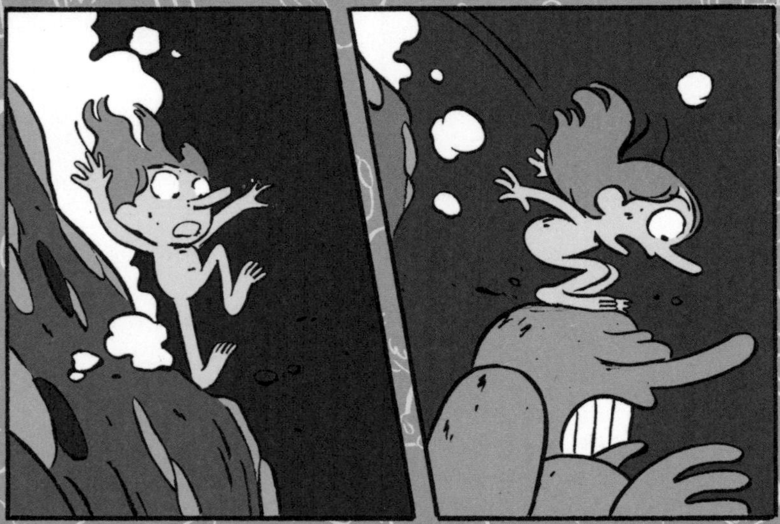

NOW, BOTH OF THEM ARE IN A RACE TO BE REUNITED BEFORE AHLBERG AND HIS SAFETY PATROL GET THE CHANCE TO USE THEIR NEW SECRET WEAPON TO DESTROY THE TROLLS, AND HILDA ALONG WITH THEM!

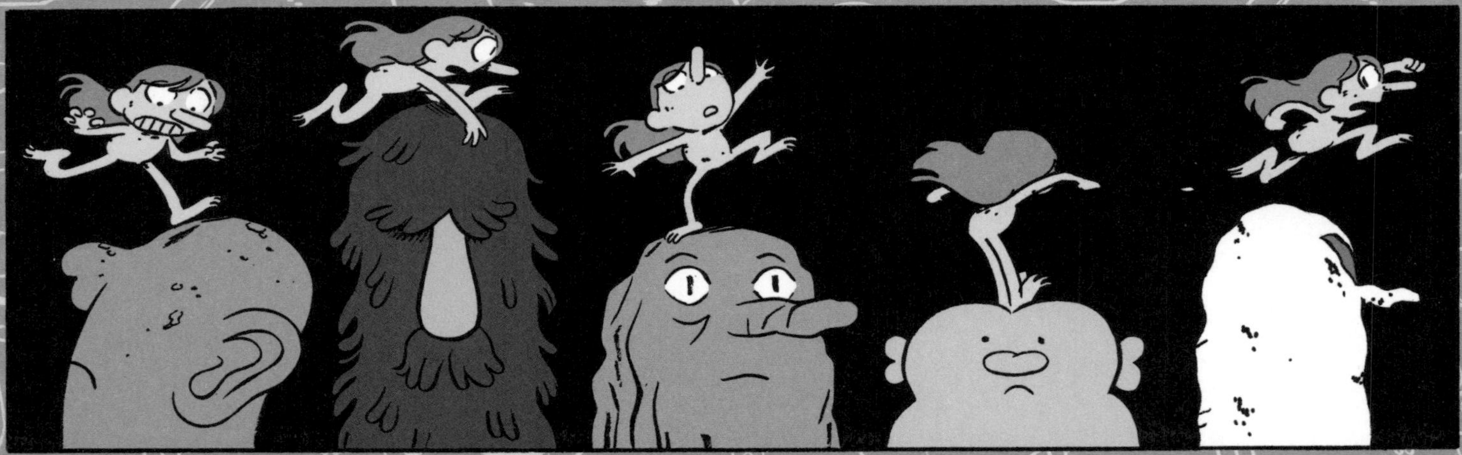

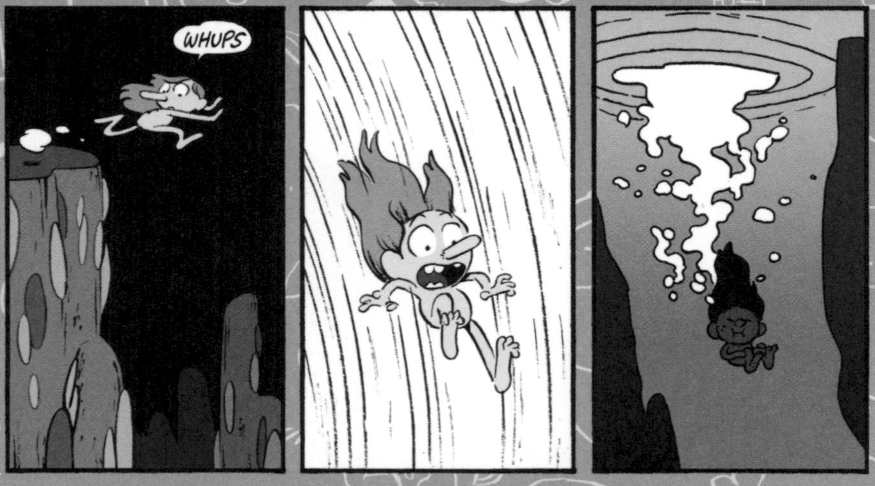
WHUPS

COMING SOON!

HILDA AND THE MOUNTAIN KING

ISBN: 978-1-911171-17-1

ORDER FROM
WWW.FLYINGEYEBOOKS.COM
OR ALL GOOD BOOKSHOPS